EVERYONE'S

BURNING

VILLARD / NEW YORK

EVERYONE'S BURNING

a novel

IAN SPIEGELMAN

Library of Congress Cataloging-in-Publication Data

Spiegelman, Ian.
Everyone's burning : a novel / Ian Spiegelman.
p. cm.
ISBN 1-40006-056-7
1. Bayside (New York, N.Y.)—Fiction.   2. Young men—Fiction.
3. Violence—Fiction.   I. Title.

PS3619.P649 E94 2003
813'.6—dc21   2002033191

Villard Books website address: www.villard.com

Printed in the United States of America on acid-free paper

24689753

First Edition

Book design by JoAnne Metsch

For Denise Orzo

". . . run your hand through the empty space it has left behind, take a last look at it, and then start moving, make sure your youth has really gone, and then calmly, all by yourself, cross to the other side of Time to see what people and things really look like."

—LOUIS-FERDINAND CÉLINE,
Journey to the End of the Night

E V E R Y O N E ' S

B U R N I N G

1

——

I knew I was getting somewhere with the drinking when the superpowers started kicking in. I was twenty-three and I didn't need to get laid anymore.

I could see things, too—black spots buzzing in the corners of my eyes, moving like gnats. I thought of them as emptinesses, as slashes in the color of the world. There was one opening up between Ortiz and me at the bar at Applebee's in the Bay Terrace shopping center. When I pointed it out he called me a maniac.

"You're beautiful," I told him.

"Have a little self-respect."

"I'm fine," taking the top off my gin and tonic, then the bottom. "See?"

"Then have a little self-respect for me."

He told me to take off my leather jacket already, he said it was summer.

"Seasons are for assholes," I told him, wiping a bead from his glass and flicking it off my thumb. The weather was going away, I said—the weather, girls, temperatures, they'd all gone off to stop mattering.

He scanned me over the rim of his glass, said, "How about a little less craziness out your mouth today?"

"I can't do it."

"On my behalf. You can do it on my behalf."

Ortiz was moving to Boise. There was opportunity in Idaho, another chance, a whole new city—he'd said it straight out. And he'd bought himself a suit to go in, black and shining, a uniform for life. He was twenty-five.

He looked good in that suit, he was beautiful, I kept staring at him. The booths around us were filled with normals in for late lunch or early dinner or whatever, breathing through their mouths and staring up at all the TV sets.

Ortiz and me had one end of the bar and Dr. Rick had the other, dozing over his glass. Back a century he might've really been a doctor, but I never got curious enough to ask. Dr. Rick was just part of the bar—he was always good for a laugh, he hated us.

Now and then I thought I heard a door opening and I'd freeze a little expecting Jeanie Riley to show up behind me. I'd been dating her for seven months without once getting into her pants. Wherever I was, Jeanie would come looking for me when she got out of class and try to take me home with her.

In the beginning she'd barely let me touch her and word had kept getting back that she was dogging me with other guys. Lately she'd been saying she was sorry, that it was hard for her to have sex with boys she really liked and that she wanted us to start over. I kept telling her I didn't belong in bedrooms anymore.

Right now, Ortiz was good to look at—

"What?" he said.

"You're a fucking ocean!"

"Excellent news."

I wouldn't be seeing it without the powers, that his eyes were so pale blue with so many gold fibers shining in them.

"I shit you not," I said.

"Would you say that if I wasn't paying for you?"

"It doesn't matter. You'll pay."

"Fucking heel."

"Pay."

A newsreader was on one of the TVs, speaking in that voice that made everything the same—

The serenity of Big Sur was now more serene than ever, a deadly morning in Trenton had ended with three dead, and two nations stood on the brink of open war.

Into my third or fourth, I turned back to Ortiz, back to the eyes, and said, "Did you hear about the open war?"

"Ah, yes," he said. "They're standing right on it."

"And it's open."

"That's big news."

"Look," I said, one of the emptinesses holding still in the corner of my eye, this place where the color of the world had torn open. "You can't move, you can't leave."

Ortiz nodded, tapping the knot of his tie.

"Look," he said.

"There's no look, I don't look—I see everything."

I meant the spots, I'd explained them, but Ortiz wasn't getting what they were.

He told me, "Drink water."

I told him again, they weren't spots, they were emptinesses.

Dr. Rick looked up when I said it, that there were slashes in the color of the world. He was an old man, almost done with his body, going through the final form—he couldn't have heard me, he was scanning.

Ortiz said, "That's excellent news, my friend. You are a giant."

A drink was coming, then it went away and then it was there again. The room was moving farther away and our temperatures were perfectly matched, mine and the room's.

"What am I going to do?" I said. "You'll leave and who do I know anymore? It'll be just the amateurs, you leave me with normals."

"Witchery," he said, "nonsense."

"Idaho's nonsense. You'll see."

Ortiz aimed his face at me, his eyes went dull.

"I woke up last night with this light on in my fucking head that I couldn't see through."

"Drink water."

The flickering red lights of the back bar made warm cherry blossoms in the brown liquors and angry devil eyes in the white ones.

"Emptinesses," Ortiz said, smiling ahead of himself, the dazzle coming back into those eyes. "You're the goods, my friend, you're the goods."

"Try not to smile so much. I can see right through your fucking head."

"A smile's a smile," hissing a sip back through the cubes. "And two ways about it there are not."

I couldn't tell whether I was feeling nice or if I wanted to hit him. He lifted his chin to me, meaning I should get happy, and the grain started wriggling in the wood of the bar.

Raising his glass to me, Ortiz said, "To the brinks of nations, to wars standing open."

"I don't toast."

When Jeanie came in I didn't know it until she was right behind me. I didn't turn around, I didn't have to—I could smell her, hear the gum snapping in her smile.

"Hey, crazy."

She looked like one of the normals from the booths—the thin white skirt, the oiled legs, white pedicure in spaghetti-strap sandals. I was embarrassed to have her around, I was afraid of her.

"Hey, hello," I said.

She leaned in for a kiss. I saw the tiny black pores across her nose, twitching like mouths, emptinesses. Her tongue against my lip sent my skin changing, it went hot, I leaned away from her.

"Shit, Leon. Would you cut it out with that?"

"Sorry."

She took the stool on my left so that I was between her and Ortiz, crossing her legs and touching my shin with the side of her foot. I moved my leg away and I could still feel her foot where she'd touched me with it.

I was trying not to look at her feet.

"So," she said, taking a lipstick and a compact from her purse, "what's going on?"

She was looking into the little mirror, holding the lipstick away from her mouth. I looked over at Ortiz and he was gone.

"You're beautiful," I told Jeanie and Ortiz popped up on the other end of the bar, sat next to Dr. Rick.

"Then be nice to me," twirling the lipstick back into its tube, snapping the compact shut.

"You have such good props for life," I said.

Jeanie smiled, put her hand on my cheek, the heat itching up through my skin. "Are you going to be nice?"

I didn't know, I moved my face away. Jeanie took her hand back, looking down at it like it might not be her hand anymore.

"Not for nothing," she said, "but you really are a fool."

"Not for nothing, but you really fucked me up."

We didn't know what to do, we stayed there, we waited.

After a while, Jeanie took a cigarette from my pack of reds on the bar and handed me my lighter to spark it for her—I liked that. I watched her smoke. She was snuffing it out when I called across the bar to Ortiz.

I said, "Come on back, Hoss. And bring your little brother with you."

Dr. Rick hated us, but he'd go where we told him to go—Ortiz paid for his drinks. Dr. Rick moved slowly, Ortiz steadying him by the shoulders, Dr. Rick's eyes half-closed, his legs shaking over each step.

"I bring the entertainment," Ortiz said, putting Dr. Rick in the stool to my right.

"Little faggots need a baby-sitter?"

"We need medical advice, Doctor."

"You need a kick in the cunt."

"Ah, Doctor," Ortiz said. "Yes, yes."

"Oh," I said, "absolutely."

"Why can't you ever be civilized?"

"Civilized?" Dr. Rick said looking her over, moving his head back a little like Jeanie was something he should be careful with. "It's civilized to dress like a little whore? I can see your pussy through that thing."

"You can suck my dick," she said. "I could get up and beat the dogshit out of you right now."

I started laughing and touched Jeanie's knee, saying, "Man lives in his circle, Doctor. It's his circle and his circle only."

"You can take that to the House of the Rising Sun in Japan," Jeanie told him, leaning out over the bar. "You can take that to the samurai."

It was all from a Charles Manson interview, Jeanie had started it with the line about the dogshit. Ortiz knew it, too—he said he didn't break laws, he made laws, he was the law*maker*.

"I make laws from here," he said, drawing a line down the middle of his chest. "Nixon was just playing on me."

Dr. Rick tried to get up, saying, "Little faggots," but with nothing between him and the earth except those broken legs of his he fell back on his stool, Ortiz steadying him by the shoulders.

"Please be careful, Doctor. We need you."

Dr. Rick said we needed to take a beating and Ortiz said, "Yes, yes, of course," tapping the bar with a plastic stirrer. "Because there's this light like all the color in the world is in my face at the same time—I can't see through it."

"You think you can teach me?" Dr. Rick said, trying to get up again. "You think you can teach me something? I'll fit all of you inside me," his shoulders shaking over the bar while his feet felt around for the floor. "I'll slap you like my son, you son of a bitch."

He went down, Ortiz and Jeanie reaching out to catch him—
I stayed where I was. From the floor, Dr. Rick shouted, "I can
fit all you little faggots inside of me," and kicked Ortiz in the
knee when he tried to touch him.

The bartender was climbing over the counter and Jeanie was
crouching down by Dr. Rick, shaking her head. I almost told
her not to touch him, but something about it needed to happen,
there was something happening that needed finishing.

She was like his mother and his daughter, reaching her hand
toward his face, whispering, and I saw him looking at that shining white curve of skin. It was too smooth, too delicate, he'd
have to tear it up—he wouldn't know what else to do with
something like that, he'd been around too long.

It must have taken all the speed Dr. Rick had left in him to
catch her, Jeanie was a quick girl, but he couldn't hold her
long—she snapped her hand out of his teeth screaming, blood
whipping away from it, and I jumped down from my stool to
grab her.

The bartender and Ortiz and one of the normals held Dr.
Rick down while he kicked out the rest of his strength. I walked
Jeanie to the kitchen, wrapped her hand in a clean rag, we went
back to the bar and drank waiting for the police.

We didn't owe anything to old men who hated us—now she
knew it too.

Ortiz's mother, that was his aunt, but he thought she was his mother until he was twelve. When someone finally told him the truth, he kept it to himself.

The story he'd always told was that him and his father were flying into Miami in 1972 when he was nine months old, that the plane crashed in the Everglades, his father died and he was raised by his mother and grandmother. Both his parents were on that plane, though—that was it for them.

There's a TV movie about the crash with the black cop from *Barney Miller* in it, that's what kind of crash it was. In one scene this baby's sitting in the wreckage, making a racket and looking around to see what's going on.

That baby, that's Ortiz.

Rahmer got the real story from their parole officer, that P.O. fucking loved to talk. Rahmer and Ortiz had blown up a car and the front door of a house when they were sixteen and they bounced around the courts for four years before they pleaded out to criminal mischief—Ortiz did a year and Rahmer did two, for being some kind of mastermind.

Once Ortiz had gone into the system anyone who worked for it could've known about his mother by turning on a computer—his lawyer had tried the Fucked Up Kid Defense and everything Ortiz ever wanted to keep to himself went right into the record, belonged to the state, forever.

Ortiz's brother—his cousin, you understand—was driving him around the day before Christmas and decided he should know, so he told him. And Ortiz, Ortiz didn't say a word, he turned to stone. His brother kept talking, told the statue of Ortiz sitting next to him that there was something like a half million dollars in trust for him, plus the house they lived in. Ortiz kept his mouth shut until they got home, then he said, "Don't ever tell anyone I know." And then he said, "Merry Christmas."

The one time I ever had the nerve to ask Ortiz about it was right after Rahmer got out and told me, when I'd been out of high school two years.

Ortiz and me were in his Eagle, out in the parking lot of the Wendy's on Northern Boulevard, waiting for this guy Lucas to show up with a gram, I turned down the volume on the CD player and just started going, I said, "That was your mom in there."

"What?"

"That plane, that was your mom. Your mom's your dad's sister—your P.O., he talks."

"What is that?" he said. "Is that conversation?"

We'd poured half the Coke out of these twenty-two-ounce cups from the drive-thru, kept all the ice, and filled them back up with Jack. I sipped mine, getting ready to talk again.

"Rahmer got it," looking out at where Northern sank down in the marsh of Alley Pond Park, where Bayside became Douglaston. "Rahmer said it, your P.O. said it—I was just wondering, I mean if you wanted you could tell me."

He moved his head back, eyed me down the bridge of his nose. "What are you fucking smoking, kid?"

I backed away from it, he had this thing his eyes did, they'd go gray and the pupils would twist smaller and smaller.

"It's conversation, it's nothing."

"Tomfoolery," he said, "nonsense."

I turned the CD back up—

Eazy-E could eat a big fat dick, Tim Dog can eat a big fat dick,
Luke can eat a fat dick . . .

Taking my reds off the dash, lighting one up, I watched my hands to keep them from shivering—I could feel it coming into my forearms, my wrists, wanting to crack my fist into the side of Ortiz's face he was giving me—his best friend my whole life and I didn't deserve to know his mother's name.

I stared out at Northern, scanning east at the flat black water stinking on either side of the lanes, the islands of saw grass, the mini-golf, Seville diner, used car lots, all of it sinking into the water.

It took years running around Bayside with Ortiz before I started seeing that it was all a swamp paved over, a few miles of houses, car washes and movie theaters in the lowlands where Little Neck Bay emptied itself—you couldn't see where the bay turned into the East River any more than you could see the mansions popping up all over it in Great Neck.

Take Northern east past Alley Pond twenty minutes and it rose up again, to more mansions, castles in Manhasset, for Persians, Russians, Indians . . . Or you could take it west twenty minutes, through the dead factories and burnt-out warehouses of Long Island City, and Manhattan shot up in your face—the gleam, the boxes of glass.

We didn't take it either way, we waited. Lucas pedaled up on his bike, Ortiz traded him through the window, handed me the plastic Baggie.

"You planning to give me anything for that?"

"You can have my fucking fist in your face if you want it."

It was a line from Buddy Rich shouting down his band, I didn't mean to start it. Ortiz was shining his eyes at me.

"We want young men—with faces," he said. "No beards."

I tried not to smile, breaking the coke up in the Baggie, crushing the clumps with my key.

"You can take that back to Sydney and do whatever the fuck they do there," Ortiz said. "I'll give you the X's on both cheeks of your life."

Taking a key-hit, I waited for the drip, kept my mouth shut. Sucking down through the ice to wash back the coke, the drink hit the numbness at the back of my throat and got caught there—I couldn't swallow, I closed my eyes.

Ortiz touched my shoulder, told me, "Take the medicine."

When I choked it down, my eyes blurred over and the drip made me queasy. Trying to get a breath, my mouth started running.

"You don't have to puke," twisting me by the shoulders until my head was out the window. "Stick the landing, kid. Stick the landing."

The air stunk from the bay, dead fish and seaweed, but it was cold at the back of my throat.

"Iron and steel, my friend," rubbing the back of my neck. "Iron and steel."

The nausea changed, it lifted, became a haze and I was back in the car, feeling solid, steady, and Ortiz nodded to show me he knew—I'd never ask about his mother again.

Trying to have friends was always a great way to get the shit kicked out of you. I was just going into high school when Rahmer and Ortiz made a fucking target out of me for every street animal that wanted to be a gangster.

That summer this piece of garbage from TMR shot three people in my driveway during a party, and another retard at another party the next week stabbed a kid in his heart and it spilled out all over Rahmer's sneakers.

TMR meant The Master Race but we all called them The Mentally Retarded. It wasn't a Nazi thing, none of those fuckers were even white—I mean, not in a way that would do you any good. They were peasants, mouth-breathers, they didn't wipe their asses. If you looked at their DNA it was all dogshit and Tic Tacs.

Even their tags were a joke, you'd see them sprayed up on all the walls—

Snot, Pest, Stain, Drone, Binki, Spic, Twinkie . . .

Still, though, they managed to kill kids and rape girls and drop dead in twos and threes just like any other gang—you had to give them that.

I could have ignored them, I'd have gone through school invisible—they shot those kids and I kept my mouth shut.

But Rahmer—that kid whose heart was pumping itself out on him said, "Why's this have to happen to me?" and Rahmer didn't know what to tell him. Then the kid was dead and Rahmer still didn't know what to tell him.

So he went and visited his father in Georgia, bought some nitrogen-based gunpowder there, and him and Ortiz made up a few pipe bombs, wrapped them with BB-laced duct tape, and picked the nearest retard's house, blew up the front door and a good hunk of the porch—plus his car.

And other cars had their windows shattered for half a mile around.

They got caught, they made the papers, and every retard at Cardozo High made me out as one of them. I stayed the hell away from Rahmer at school, told the retards I hardly knew him when they got in my face, but now and then I'd take a beat-down anyway.

There was this sound they made before they jumped you, this rumbling coming up through the asphalt that had you twisting around trying to see what direction it was coming from. But it never mattered where it came from. By the time you heard it coming it was already there—you couldn't stop it coming.

Three of them tried Rahmer once out by the bleachers but it cost them so much that they never got the nerve up again—down where they looked for themselves, they were all little girls. But Rahmer, something was so fucked in him. We went at it a few times and I still have the feeling that if he hadn't decided I was the wrong person to take it out on someone would've had to cut his head off before he'd let go of my neck.

And Ortiz? That fucking pussy transferred to some mongoloid underachiever private school in Flushing, kept clear of TMR altogether, never showed his face. All he had to do was cool it while his lawyer worked out his trial, his appeal. He'd spend lunch picking up Korean girls out on Main Street and Northern and I'd be hiding out in study hall watching the poindexters drool on their notebooks.

Still, I'd show up anytime Ortiz called—who else was there? We'd hang out in his basement popping mesc or acid and watch *Friday the 13th 3D*, *21 Jump Street*—cracking up at jokes that weren't there, making Ouija boards, trying to get the devil to say

something. Whatever he was up to, Ortiz was just smiling away
like a bastard. Waiting out that trial, it was summer all the time
for him—he never thought they'd send him up.

Me, I didn't know what they'd do and I didn't think about it.
I kept my fucking head down at school, hung out at Ortiz's, and
if it popped into my head that he'd made my life a piece of shit
I popped it back out again just as quick.

It wasn't as easy with Rahmer. He was enough of a madman
to come up with the idea in the first place, there's no ignoring
that much hate coming off a person. I always wanted to tell him
to fuck off once and for all but I couldn't get myself there—he
hated all the right things.

Ortiz's beating finally caught up with him a few weeks after I graduated. We were having beers in the yard at P.S. 203 one night, just talking shit, and there was that rumbling, the sneakers pounding asphalt.

Holy fuck, the dance they did on him—George Tatsis, Frankie Venages, and a bunch of their boys. I didn't stick around, Tatsis nailed me in the face and I started booking, got past the fence and turned around to see where Ortiz was. He was back there under the hoop trying to reason with Venages, holding up his hands screaming, "I got no beef with you!" and letting that kid smash him in the face with all the other retards coming up in the dark.

Up at Springfield and Horace Harding I called 911 and threw up in the phone booth from running. The response was too late to help Ortiz but he named three of the punk-asses that jumped him and the cops arrested them out of their houses over the next couple of days. I heard that Venages busted out crying in front of his cop father when they came—I liked that.

But then this detective calls me at my mom's place and tells me I have to come down to the 111th to I.D. them. When I said no, Ortiz called me up saying this could help his appeal, make him look like a victim and maybe the judge takes it easy on him, decides not to send him up. That was bullshit, and I said so, but Ortiz swore it would help.

So I told the cop okay, but I wasn't going to the station. I said, "I work nights, Detective. I work in the kitchen at Uno's and it's hot in there. This is my free time—I'm air-conditioned in here."

"Mr. Koch," he said, and that meant for me to go fuck myself. "This is going to take five minutes. These gentlemen cracked three of your buddy's ribs. They broke his nose. You're not interested in helping him?"

"These gentlemen—you know them, you have them. Ortiz
named them. You have them." I put my cheek on the kitchen
table, trying to cool my face, and closed my eyes. It spun too
much in the dark and I opened my eyes again. "What's good for
not throwing up, Detective? I'm sick."

"I need you to come down here, Mr. Koch."

"You don't need me," I said. "I told you I have no license, I
can't drive—you can come here, you're licensed. Come arrest
me, I'm sick, you can take me away."

Two of them showed up and I recognized the older one—I
was scared of him.

We were walking into the living room with me going backward up the steps in front of the detectives. The older one gave
me Polaroids to look at of Venages, Tatsis, and Botch, but I
didn't want to look away from his face.

We stopped in the middle of the room and the younger one
was talking. "Yeah, this is the house," he said. He was looking
around at the orange walls, the blue carpet, smiling, laughing at
it. "You had a little party here a few years ago? A little shoot 'em
up party?"

I kept my eyes on the older cop. He was the one who wrote
the report when I got grabbed in the ravine by school in second
grade. I was afraid he was going to move.

"That was you, right?"

"That wasn't me," I said. "That was my brother—it was his
party. I was fourteen."

"Do you know what happens to someone when they get shot
in the stomach?" the younger cop said. "Do you know that a
person's stomach expands after he's shot? Like a balloon?"

"You have a gun," I said. "Show me."

"You don't need me to do that." He was speaking at the side
of my face.

The older cop reached out toward me and I stepped back to make a space between us. Even if I couldn't stop him from crossing it, I could show him that I meant to put the space there and that it would mean something if he crossed it.

The pictures were fanned out in my hands like playing cards and he tapped one of them with his finger.

"So, Mr. Koch. Do you know these guys?"

I wouldn't look down. I didn't want him to come forward or move away. He had to stay still—everyone had to stay where they were.

"Mr. Koch?"

I said their names with my eyes on the detective—Frankie Venages, Anthony Botch, George Tatsis. He held out his hand for the Polaroids and I didn't move. He had to take them out of my hands and I stayed like I was, kept my hands where they were.

"Your friend's getting beaten half to hell," the other one said, "and you take off running," shaking his head in the corner of my eye, shaking the whole idea of me out of his head—out of everyone's heads.

"It was better that way," I told the older one. "If I'd have tried to do anything we would've had to watch each other getting fucked up like that."

"That's one way of looking at it."

He put the pictures back in his jacket. They were leaving. The younger one went out first and the older one was almost out the door but I stopped him. He couldn't just leave, I couldn't just let him. He couldn't just walk out and get in a car and drive, make arrests, write reports—eat dinner and sleep. I could see him doing all that, working, sleeping at night—doing everything. Because all of that was what anyone wanted and he could just go do it.

He turned around in the foyer looking at me. I'd told him to stop, I'd said, "Wait a minute—no."

Neither of us said anything. I could hear the buzzing of all the machines in the house like someone was humming in my ear, vibrating the tiny bones inside, making my whole body quiver, down to the cells—wanting them to come apart.

"You know me," I said.

He changed his face at me, scrunched it up, making me out.

"You grabbed my wrist," I said. "I didn't want to look at any more pictures so you grabbed my wrist."

He kept changing his face—he couldn't make me out, I was unbelievable to him.

"What do you mean I grabbed your wrist? I haven't touched you."

"Not these pictures. Not pictures of kids. There weren't any kids—it was just me. I didn't want to look at any more pictures because all the men were the same and I didn't want to know any of them."

"Hey, hey, slow down," he was saying, his arm coming up, slow, with his hand on the end of it, moving toward my shoulder. I looked at his hand like it had to stop coming before it got to me and he took it away, hooked his thumb into his pants pocket and left it hanging there.

I told him how I'd been crying and telling him to close the book, that when I got up to run he'd grabbed my wrist and pulled me back to the desk.

"It was like everyone in the station was watching me," I said. "My mother was there—I was supposed to let her see his face? I was supposed to show her what he *looked* like?"

He did this whole thing—looking at me from one angle and another, nodding and stroking his chin like what he had to say was taking time to dawn on him. He said, "You were supposed to show me."

"Fucking cops," I said. "What, now you know me?"

He nodded, serious—he had serious things to say.

"As far as I know, we never caught the guy. We brought in a lot of freaks but none of them ever linked up."

"I guess you're not a very good cop."

He smiled, shrugging me off, leaned back against the door-way. "Fair enough," he said. "Anything else?"

"Yeah," my throat going hot, my eyes trying to close them-selves. "Yeah, okay," but I couldn't think of what to say.

He was scanning me, hard, his face wrinkling up with want-ing to help, the whole thing, squinting at me like something was coming into him that would settle everything between everyone once and for all.

"You've got a lot of junk floating around in your head there, my friend."

There was no point in talking—I felt stupid, I felt six years old. That's what it meant, talking to cops. This cop, though, he wouldn't shut his mouth.

"Maybe you think this freak is still out there," he said. "Maybe he is. We can't know, my friend. All I can tell you is that if you feel like you should have done more—well, you don't have to feel that way."

I didn't say a thing, he wasn't getting anything.

"It's been a long time," coming into my space, hands on his belt, leaning down a little so that we were eye to eye. Breathing through my nose I could smell him. I breathed through my mouth and tasted him.

"Look," he said. "Who knows? Maybe you come down and look at some mug shots—I'll work with you. Maybe something clicks. It's worth a shot."

If I didn't start talking, he wouldn't stop—all of them had that.

So I said, "I'm hearing you," turning, giving him the back of my head. I went and sat across the foyer from him, on the bot-tom step. "I'm hearing you," I said.

"Are you?"

"Yep. It's been so long though. Let me ask you—what do you think about a person like that?"

"What do I think? I think we need to lock him up."

"No, I mean, someone like that—you think he's gotten better by now or you think he's getting worse?"

He didn't say anything, so I went back to him, stood so close you couldn't fit another person between us. I was thinking he could punch me or grab me or lick my face. I was so scared the corner of my mouth started twitching when I spoke. But I stayed there, I kept talking.

"I bet you he's a lot worse by now. The shit he's up to by now has got to be so bad that I practically want to thank him. I mean, the way I'm feeling I'm thinking like I want to go and thank him for letting me off easy."

"Look," he said.

"And I'm thankful to you, too," I said. "Maybe I should do something to thank you? You want to make me thank you?"

I saw his head flick backward, his head and shoulders, I felt a click go through me—I'd cost him something.

"Go ahead," I said. "Make me thank you. You can if you want."

He said "Look" again, stepping back and shaking his head, trying to find something. But there was nothing there for him to find—everything was mine. "Look," he said, "you've got a lot of stuff going on."

"I don't have anything going on."

"Listen," he said, "listen. A case like yours—"

"It's not mine, it's yours. I never had it, it's yours—it's your case. Go read it, go jerk off on it. You can if you want."

He said something, he left, I felt like shit—it doesn't matter what he said.

I just sat there on the step, trying to figure out what I wanted to say. I kept picturing that report. I imagined it in the dark somewhere, locked up in a filing cabinet in that shining white precinct tucked in with all those blurry mug shots of monsters.

It seemed to me that any of those faggots would get a hard-on just knowing how close their faces were to such a nasty piece of kiddie porn. And if decent people ever saw it—decent people would puke till their eyes bled. That's why they had it locked up, because there were only the two kinds of people. And me.

I was a little piece of porn.

2

_____

They went, they were gone—six hours upstate in a town I'd never heard of. Rahmer had seen it coming, he made himself ready in his head, didn't say a word for weeks. Ortiz, though— that silly prick dreamed himself all the way to the sentencing and that beat-down hadn't bought him a thing. He could've gotten slit nuts to neck and the state would've made his fucking corpse serve the time.

Me, I got what I could out of it. There was this girl I was all wrapped up in, this girl Dara. We hung out a lot but she never let me touch her until Ortiz and Rahmer got sent up.

She was the hostess at the Uno's on Bell Boulevard when I was doing salad prep, she was tiny and boyish but what really did it to me was her lazy black eye—always drifting off on its own, looking for something. And she was the fussiest little bitch I'd ever met. I guessed she was my kind from the way she kept sending people to hell every chance she'd get—telling delivery guys to shut up and wait outside, snapping at busboys, keeping one waitress begging for customers while she gave another more than she could handle.

She'd get on the intercom, telling me, "You better be kidding—get that shit out here _now_," and I'd tell her to fuck off, with the feeling screaming around in me that the best thing I could ever do with myself would be to beg her for something, really beg her, on my knees—talking fast to her with my throat hurting, kissing her stupid Pumas.

But I never thought it would happen. After work we'd go up to her apartment—both her parents were doctors and they kept sending money no matter what she did—we'd get wasted, and the girl couldn't stop telling me how she hated people touching her, that she only liked girls and that she'd only liked a few girls in her life but that she only really liked one of them.

Then my best friends went to prison, it made the change.

We were up at her place, we were doing coke, being morbid, talking about who was more fucked up. I told her how I felt with the guys gone, how alone—danced it around in front of her lazy eye until she was ready to twist the whole room for me. I could see her face changing, the drift-eye shivering and the other one opening up at me. I told her about the faggot in the ravine, down in the woods—I told her everything.

She was crying, she sniffed it back, leaned down for a line and when she came back up the drip from her nose was climbing over her lip. I wiped it away with my thumb—hand jittering, the pulse bouncing up against the little curving space under her nose and back up through my fingers, all through my arm, hot, into my face.

"Your cheeks are all red," she said.

"I like touching you."

"Do it again."

Even with my hand on her cheek, even with her eye on me—the only one that ever looked at anything dead-on—I kept thinking I'd never get there, that she'd pull away. But she leaned her face toward me and then I had both hands on her cheeks with her hair coming forward, touching the tops of my fingers. I spoke to myself—

That's Dara's hair—Dara's—the little screamer, the lesbian—that's Dara's hair and her cheeks—and these are my fingers touching them.

And that was Dara's tooth and those were her teeth and it was my tongue touching them. She was kissing me harder and harder, shoving me onto my back while she climbed on top of me, choking me with her tongue until her spit was running down my cheeks.

"Kiss me like that," she said. "Don't kiss me nice."

Something shot past the corner of my eye, this little flurry of darkness—I turned to see what it was and Dara yanked my face to hers.

"Look at me."

"Okay."

"Look at me."

"I am."

She shook her head no, she put her hand on my throat—there were lights all over her face, bursts of red and yellow, the blue glow of the TV.

"Listen."

If I wanted to be with her, she said, I couldn't be a boy, I had to do better than that. She told me what it meant, we traded ideas, tried a few things—it didn't take long before we'd worked it down to a system.

Dara would stop me after four drinks to be sure I could do my part when we got around to actually having sex—it was surefire, we were like a machine together, she knew what she was doing.

I tried to quit once, I tried to bail out—we were working away on each other and by two or three in the morning I was so hungry I lost my place. When it started I didn't even realize what it was, couldn't recognize it—my stomach burning away and my mouth starting to run, wanting to take something apart.

I'd have gone around the corner to the 7-Eleven and gotten one of those imitation Egg McMuffins you heat up in the microwave but, the thing is, Dara's ass was in my face. It's not like her ass was in the way or anything—I mean, you understand, I was licking it. Because I was her kid brother and if I didn't do it she'd tell Mom how she'd caught me jerking off in the toolshed.

"You disgust me," she was saying in her southern accent. "You just downright make me sick, you little pervert—don't you stop!"

What did the normals do with themselves—play soccer, think about law schools? What's soccer? Schools of law?

Dara reached around, swatting me across the face, told me to go faster, and backhanded, cheek singing, I went faster.

"Slow down, motherfucker!"

We lived on this farm down in Texas—that's why we had the toolshed in the first place. Dara liked doing the voice, she loved to say "motherfucker" as this bratty little Texan girl.

"Keep going, motherfucker. Don't you stop. I'll tell. I swear by the Lord I'll tell."

We were Baptists, we name-dropped the Lord all the time—it was cool doing that.

"You are in so much trouble, boy."

It was true—there was the whole night ahead of me and I was already getting dizzy from wanting some food. Dara was growling out her lines but I was having a hard time staying in the game. So many parts hadn't happened yet and there was no part in it where I could get anything to eat—you understand, anything else.

"Slow down, motherfucker! Lick me slower." I slowed down, licked her slower, Dara shaking her head, saying, "Filthy, filthy, filthy."

Any second now I'd be going too slow, and then too fast again. Of course, there was no way to do it right, no way to be good, but I had to toss Dara's salad just right or there'd be trouble. Trouble? Do it right or skin would fry, be good, keep the demons in hell— keep the Lord away. The Lord's coming— hurry, motherfucker! It's coming! Quick now!

"Go faster, stupid! Are you really that stupid? Hurry up!"

Next came the part where I was supposed to admit I liked it and start begging her to let me keep doing it—telling her how beautiful she was and how much I loved all the dirty parts of her body. Then, together or almost together, we'd come.

After that it would be Dara's turn—me being, say, a teacher who could fail her or some stranger that'd snatched her up off the street. See, we both wanted the same role.

"You just love my ass, don't you, boy?"

I did. But I hadn't been food-hungry in so long that it came to me hard, that hollowness rolling over itself in my stomach, throwing fire at the bottom of my throat. And there was still so much to do.

"No!" I said, in as young a voice as I could make.

"Don't you dare lie to me," reaching around and pulling me to her by the hair. "If there's one thing the Lord hates it's a little liar. Now tell me you love it, motherfucker!"

I could feel my stomach vibrating in the hinge of my jaw while my tongue reached out for her. The whole thing was rising up, begging me to put something in it, so I pulled my head back, brought my palm up, and brought it back hard—flat across one cheek of her ass.

"Oh," she said, turning around, lowering her head a little. "Is Leon improvising?"

Leon was trying to get a bagel. There was no way I'd ever make it out of there without Dara getting her turn, so I was jumping right into it.

"You've been bad," I said, getting up from my knees. "You are in a lot of trouble, young lady."

"Me?" she pouted, putting her hands behind her back. "But I'm good."

I shook my head no—two shakes, two beats per shake—one-two, tick-tock.

"What did I do bad?"

It wasn't her voice anymore, it was higher now, smaller—a scared little kid, her breath trembling under the words.

"You don't know? You don't remember what you did? Well, you'd better start thinking about it. Think about what you did."

"But I don't remember."

That was enough whining, I told her. "Do you really think that if you pout enough and give me those sad little baby eyes I'll let you walk away like nothing happened?"

She didn't say anything, my stomach made some noise, and Dara got on her knees—I hated seeing that, but the one time I'd complained, Dara had smashed the bathroom window with a bottle of Drano.

"Are you really that stupid, girl?"

Her head shook no—one-two.

"You're not?"

Tick-tock.

Well. Now she was just plain lying and we both knew how the Lord felt about liars. She had to be kidding me—she knew what she did, she remembered—everyone told her—even if they didn't know, they told her and she knew it. And she'd admit it, right this second—now!—or there'd be trouble.

It was one thing to be stupid, but we came down hardest on the liars.

"You better start thinking about it, little girl."

"No!"

No? Did she just say no? I had to light a cigarette for this.

Her eyes were getting bigger, darker, her face going red and her breath making the words quiver—

"But I'm a good girl!"

If she was so good, then why was this happening? Could she answer that? Of course she couldn't, she was too stupid.

"Or are you just a little liar? It's one or the other, young lady, because it'll never be both."

"Hurry," in her own voice, looking up from her knees, rubbing herself.

"Okay, okay."

As I was walking her out the bedroom, to the couch, Dara said, "Damn it, Leon, put that out," so I went back into the bedroom, snuck another drag, and snuffed it. Back in the living room, I couldn't believe the couch was still so far away, that I still had her by the hair, was still dragging her to it. Then we finally got there, I finally pulled her across my lap telling her she was getting what she deserved, but—fuck!—we hadn't even started yet.

A spanking isn't just a couple whacks on the ass and then you get to go have a Pepsi. These things have rhythm, these things take time. I had to let my hand hover, bounce it in the space above her so she felt the air moving—tap, make her wait for it, stroke her back with the other hand—so she knew I was there, so she had to wait for it.

The room was looking watery, my head filling up with air and all these gripe-noises coming out of my stomach. But I still had to do everything, all of the slapping, the spanking, the smacking—plus the hover and tap in between—slowly—and then speed up—three smacks, four in a row—four, five—then slow down, hover and tap, get fast again—five, six in a row—six, seven—

"Don't lie to me, you little slut!"

Egg McMuffins—Jesus, I loved those things. They were so warm and soft, salty . . . Sausage McMuffin with Egg—even better, with that cheese melting over the sausage, the egg kind of popping in your teeth . . .

But we were so just in the beginning of it, it wasn't even the beginning of the middle—I'd barely put a shine on that ass. There I was hovering, asking her who was right.

"Me," she said, so I had to reach down and yank her hair, hiss at her, call her a liar—or was she just stupid?

"No!"

"Say it!"

Oh, we'd be at this all night if she wanted. It didn't matter if I was starving because it wasn't over until she said it was, until she admitted that I was right—that she was a stupid little slut, a liar—that she was bad. And she absolutely wouldn't do that until she had all the commotion going, the screaming and crying and the "Please look at me!"

"This is what you get," at top speed. "Do you hear me? This is what little liars get."

I couldn't even hope for a break, something to nibble, a little refreshment—hell no. Like there'd be food in that anorexic refrigerator of hers? Food?

7-Eleven was right around the corner.

"Pay attention!"

"I'm sorry. I'm just really hungry."

"Are you for real?" she said.

I wasn't even close to being for real. I said, "What do you want from me—I'm starving. Some of us like to eat food once in a while."

She said she couldn't believe me and rolled over, stretching out on the couch, her legs over mine, squinting at me in the dark.

"Look at me."

"I'm looking right at you, princess."

Each word was high and sharp, it was her teacher voice, her getting-near-a-fight voice.

"If I am naked and you are thinking about something else," her toes crawling up my chest, pinching a nipple, "I will absolutely kill you. Does that sound fair?"

"Oh, absolutely."

Her head went no—tick-tock. She wanted convincing, wanted to hear me say more things. Forget being slapped around and pretending she was being forced to give a blow job she was giving—talking's what really got her. She leaned her face forward, watching me through the tops of her eyes, the steady one beaming into me while the other one drifted away.

I said the things I always said. But I'd never heard them so sober before—

Ah, wasn't she great but, more important, wasn't it great how we understood each other? And even better than all that wasn't it, like, critical?—like we were at the heart of something and it was something we made ourselves? Wasn't it just the two of us and death to all outsiders because no one else would ever get it?

"World?" I said. "What world? It's just us because we understand each other and we understand each other so it's just us. And we never forget it, we never forget each other—we never forget anything."

My stomach was making a fucking feast out of itself. I was so dizzy Dara's eyes were going in and out of her face and the room kept getting darker and darker while I kept talking about us, kept going—

We, we, we, us, us, us, you, you, you, me, me, me . . .

"But, fuck, Dara, there is a world. And there's food in it!"

She smiled, wriggling onto my lap. "Look at me."

"Listen, princess, listen," I said. "Can't you hear the racket going on in there? There's a whole motherfucking orchestra in there—listen to it."

Tick-tock. "Stop being a baby, Leon."

"It's a concert in there, Dara. Hear it? The horns? All that brass? There are cymbals in there, there are drums!"

Dara watched me for a second, scanning me with the steady eye, the one that was in this world. Then she bent down, pressing the side of her face to my stomach.

"Damn," she giggled. "That's crazy."

"I know. What do you think I'm telling you?"

"I can hear it."

"Of course you can."

"But, sweetie," she said, kissing me. "Don't you know how they end symphonies?"

"Um?" I shrugged.

She was whispering into my mouth, breathing into me.

They'd set off rockets and cannons before it was over, she said. We'd get to see everything light up, the both of us, the sky catching fire, choking—all the people and buildings and houses glowing in the dark, and us too.

She pressed her lips together and the lazy eye focused on me for the first time, its lid shivering. She cupped my jaw in her hands.

"Everything has to be burning."

Dara's voice was two sounds at once—the one you heard first, that made the words, and the one rolling underneath it that told you what she meant, how she was feeling. And I had to listen close to what the undersound was doing since the words that came out of her fucking mouth stopped making any sense at all after a while—she kept saying two things at the same time, like "I love you, Leon, but we have to stop playing with each other."

If she said it with a giggle underneath, it meant she was just doing some girl from a movie who tells the guy "We have to stop meeting like this!" and I'd pinch her ass or she'd hop up on my face and we'd make our machine, go into our system.

When she said it dark down the bridge of her nose, though, it meant we were going to fight about it. She'd tell me, "It's just wrong—it's, like, *born* wrong to treat each other like that. Even if we want it," and I'd ask what the hell she'd been talking about with all that fire shit that night. Dara would bust out crying, I'd get as drunk as I wanted in her kitchen and pass out on the couch after she went to bed. Then I wouldn't see her for weeks.

Rooms would get smaller, my breath would keep catching in my throat—I'd get drunk and I'd stay there.

Aside from Dara, the only person I spent any time with was Rahmer's girlfriend, this girl Cali. And aside from Rahmer and me, Cali didn't know anyone at all—she was too good-looking, people couldn't see a way in with her. Guys would try to fuck her, it's all they could come up with, and they'd hate her for being out of their class. Girls, they hated her just on sight, just for the face she was born with.

When Rahmer was doing his bid I'd keep her company but it was hard—I got nervous just looking at her face.

We'd be walking down Bell and if I fell back a step some motherfucker would pop up out of nowhere and start walking next to her, trying to catch a rap. Everyone, it didn't matter what they looked like, everyone took their chances on Cali— they knew they'd get blown off, they just couldn't stop themselves. Me, though, I stopped myself. I'd pretend to be her boyfriend and I'd stop myself.

When some dude came up on her, I'd slip myself between them, grab Cali's hand and want to throw up—she was so much.

It wasn't just Cali's face that made me afraid of her, something was fucked inside her too. She had this cold in her, this thing that kept everything away and she didn't even have to work on it—I wanted a part of it.

We were supposed to go up with Rahmer's mom for a visiting day and Cali pulled out at the last second, said she couldn't blow off her classes. She showed up at my mom's place the night before with a bag of jelly beans, wanting me to give it to him.

"Jelly beans?" I said. "You fucking send jelly beans?"

I had the same Faith No More song playing over and over again on a loop—

Go on and wring my neck like when a rag gets wet a little
discipline for my pet genius . . .

Cali turned it off, telling me, "He likes them." She went and sat on my bed, I closed the door. "I call him my jelly bean— get it?"

"Sure."

"He won't like it."

"That's true."

She said she had class tomorrow, she said, "What am I supposed to do?"

"I guess you send jelly beans."

I sat next to her and turned on the TV. Cali took the remote from me and started flipping stations.

"It's okay if I hang out?"

"Yeah."

She kicked off her sneakers, lay across my bed on her stomach, her feet up by my shoulder, me watching the shadows shift in the wrinkles of her arches, the light bending on the backs of her thighs. She had her ass peeking out the bottom of her shorts, she was unreal—even staring right at her I couldn't imagine what she was.

She said, "They're not giving anything."

"What?"

"On TV—they're not giving anything."

"Sorry."

She curled her toes, her ass was like a beating heart—I could see myself licking the sweat off it, I kept my mouth shut, tried to look at something else, she smiled back at me over her shoulder.

"You love my feet."

"Fuck you."

All through it, Rahmer had me on collect calls every chance he got.

The state machine would say in a woman's voice, "Hello. You have received a collect call from," and Rahmer would jump in spitting, "It's me," low and fast, sounding embarrassed to be who he was. Then the state would finish, "an inmate at a New York State correctional facility. Hang up to decline the call or to accept dial one now."

It could get up to forty, fifty dollars some months, but there was nothing you could say about it—they had him, I was outside, so everything was supposed to be perfect for me.

Cali, she maxed out at 250 one month, her dad took her phone away, and I got to hear all about it from both ends.

Ortiz, he never made a collect call in his life.

There were letters, too, every week, twice a week, I couldn't write back fast enough. It was Rahmer and his rights, you couldn't stop hearing about them—he talked civics, he talked history, the law—everything he was learning locked down, on and on, forever.

I started taking classes at Queens College and Rahmer writes me about how easy I had it, how I'd never learn real history in a fucking college, not in this country—a country had to be judged by its prisons.

I wrote back saying not to quote me any more Jesus freaks, that he could fuck himself, and then I stopped hearing from him.

"He's really hurt," Cali told me. We were out back at her folks' place up in Rye and it was getting dark—she was making me fly a kite with her little brothers.

"What can I do about that?"

"Just say you're sorry."

"I'm not though."

"You have to be."

Both her brothers were running away from us, tugging the string, trying to get each other to let go while this tiny red diamond looped and snagged in the air.

She said it again, that I had to be sorry, and I told her I didn't have to be anything.

"Maybe you've got nothing to do except write prison letters," I said, "but I don't have that kind of time."

"They're not prison letters. They're just letters, they're just regular human letters like anyone sends anyone."

She was holding the collar of her denim jacket closed, the wind flipping her hair back from her face. Cali's face was cut so clean, so even, it was like no one had ever touched it. I watched it from different angles, new things kept showing up in it—something made me touch my cheek.

"Maybe I don't need to fucking baby-sit you anymore."

"Now you hurt me too," she said. "What else can you do?"

I stopped in the grass and Cali was walking away. I watched the kite swirling over her head, that red diamond making circles in the air—the circles vibrated, they were inside each other. There was something like a gnat buzzing in my eye, the kite stood still and the sky spun behind it. I lit a cigarette, I waited.

News cameras shot us from helicopters—Dara and me, her little socialist pals, plus another twenty, thirty thousand City U. students. They used the shots to count us up, multiplying heads per square foot—we found out later.

Dara made me go, I didn't want anything to do with it—there was nothing in the city I wanted any part of, just yuppies and foreigners, dead weight, rich homos calling us bridge and tunnel.

But there we were, you can check the papers—Union Square, maybe one in the afternoon—that was us, that was me, I was getting a baton in the shoulder, Dara took it in the face. And then everyone pounding asphalt, bent over, covering our faces from the invisible cloud of pepper spray, the burning air.

I knew everything that happened before it happened, because of the odds—all those kids with no business outside their houses waving their fists at cops. They'd loaded our group onto buses back in Queens and I could see what the rest of the day was going to be like—the wall of cops on both sides of us, three officers thick, then five, then ten—a wall on the east and a wall on the west, us heading south, forward—an army of heads all pointing in the same direction, toward City Hall, screaming, fists in the air.

"You say cut back! We say fuck that!"

All these chants, I remember them—

"The people! United! Will never be defeated!"

I told Dara it didn't even rhyme and she rolled her eyes. "What's up your ass?" I screamed—you couldn't hear a thing except the mob and the bullhorns. Dara smacked me across the face, she'd never done it in public before—I didn't know how I felt about it.

There was a shiver down in my solar plexus, a cold strobe of panic, it went hot shooting up through my neck, hotter behind my eyes—I had to shut them against it. When I opened them up the air was humming with tiny dots, black vacuums between all the faces.

I looked at Dara and she was already looking away, stretching her neck and getting up on her toes, trying to find Justin's hair through all the other heads and shoulders.

All you need to know about Justin, you understand, is that he was a white kid with dreadlocks. He'd helped organize the Queens College group, he liked to organize things. Dara had lost him in the crowd somewhere.

We could have been fifty, sixty thousand—I remember seeing us on the news, the column of heads, fifty across, east-west, and north to south forever, waving the banners, walled in by cops— full riot gear, the visors and the plastic shields. The news gave a number but I don't remember it, just what we looked like.

White kids had their fists up like footage of Black Panthers— Dara too, shaking knuckle and bone—the same act for thirty years.

"You say cut back! We say fuck that!"

That slap in the face, it didn't make a sound, no one heard a thing. Everyone was aiming their faces at something they couldn't see—City Hall. We'd been walking an hour and there was still no sign of it, except that the cops were getting thicker around us, ten deep, fifteen. I thought City Hall was a dream, a castle they made up to keep people walking—there was something in it if you just kept moving, scream, wave a sign at it—

SUBVERT THE DOMINANT PARADIGM

EDUCATION IS A RIGHT NOT A PRIVILEGE

Show a magic sign and the castle would pop up, gates swinging open—angels would fly out.

We'd never get there, though. We were bottlenecked at Union Square.

"The people! United!"

There was no City Hall, the cops would get us, crack our bones, let out the pepper cloud—I wanted to tell them.

"Hurry, Leon!"

"Where? I can't move!"

And anywhere I turned something hit me—elbows, the backs of heads, all these kids with their interesting haircuts, always getting closer to those cops. Someone would touch one of those shields—that'd do it.

"Leon!" dragging me by the wrist. I'd been stumbling, watching it. That's what I'd really come for, to see it happen, see those black batons come down on all of that fascinating hair—spiked, curled, coiffed, twisting in dreads. The only surprise was when they hit me too—I thought they'd notice that I was just there to see it. I mean, the cops and me, we had the same look on our faces.

"You fucking pigs!" Dara screamed.

"Jesus, Dara! Get away from them—don't even look at them!"

"Pigs!" It tore up her throat.

Dara had it worse than anyone, had to be the first one at the castle—something was in it for her, all the windows would shine, warm her face, she had to get there.

"Motherfuckers!" eyes wide and shining, the lazy one on the drift. She couldn't get at them, though, stuck in the middle of the column. They couldn't even see her. But it wouldn't last—someone had planned the day for us, volunteered us. There was one of them now, there was Justin.

"Justin, wait!"

He was up ahead of us, maybe ten bodies away from the police-wall to the east, waving his sign at the cops—so they could see it.

"Justin!" She was calling his name, using her mouth to make his name—Justin, this white boy with dreads.

When they started swinging on us, all Justin ended up getting was a tap in the eye—it wasn't enough to show him anything, he never figured out why he was there.

Dara towed me through the mob, toward Justin, the shields just past his shoulder, shoving people out of the way with her free hand, ducking through gaps between the bodies.

When we got to Justin he said, "Oh, there you are," and Dara got perky, smiling. She said, "Here I am."

Justin put his free hand on the top of Dara's arm, the other hand holding a sign—the sign said there was a paradigm, that it was dominant, and that it needed subverting. This bitch knew so much about subverting paradigms that he even had a black friend—there he was, this kid Kenny, who wasn't really all that black. Kenny, he had a sign too—it made fun of the mayor's name.

Seventy, eighty thousand cunts—it was something to see. In a few minutes they'd toss me at the cops. Those cops were closer and closer, jaws tight behind the tops of their shields, squinting through their visors, batons shouldered.

Those cops were full of potential.

And any second now someone would tap plastic, nudge a shield, and it would be like tripping a bear trap. We couldn't stop it happening—a hundred thousand punk-asses with hairstyles and ideas.

I saw a sign that said Kent State was a place to remember. That was Sharon Keys holding it, my History of Progress professor— she wore fishnets to class, even the girls wanted to fuck her.

The column was going forward, south, while the space ahead

got smaller and smaller, the two cop-walls closing in. Some of us were twisting inside the mob, trying to stop, stand still, go back. But the crowd carried us, begging to hit a button, bring the clubs down. It's like they were itching inside for something hard to crush their muscles against their bones, give them marks to show off—new rights.

"You say cut back! We say . . ."

It was Dara's voice saying that—they'd taught her new things to say, new ways to use her mouth.

"The people! United!"

She was cutting through the column, cutting east, squeezing head and shoulders through the bodies, stretching her neck toward the cops. I pulled her back, she twisted her wrist away, shoved herself back into the bodies—just arm's length from the plastic shields. Justin, Justin was sucking bullhorn—

"People! People!" he said. Then he said other things, things that sounded like, *I'm an angel! Wheee! I'm an angel!*

He never got anything, just a jab in the eye—nothing.

I was three or four bodies behind Dara in this kind of semicircle facing off with the cops, Dara screaming for them to fuck themselves, Justin right next to her telling his bullhorn he was an angel.

Other people had things to say, too. They sounded like—

Wheee! My dad's partner went down on me every chance he got the whole year I was nine! Wheee! My parents give me money and we'll never talk about it! Wheee! Beat the dirty out of me!

Wheee! I'm black! My father's got a Lexus and my voice isn't black enough! Wheee! Beat the white out of me!

Wheee! My brother lost his eyes in Vietnam! I was marching then too! Wheee! I'm always doing this! Wheee! Beat the marching out of me!

I kept my mouth shut. If I'd said anything it would've sounded like, "I'm with Dara."

So it finally started happening. First, Justin stepped into the space between the front of our half circle and the body-wall, touched a shield with his bullhorn while he screamed into it, got his little nudge in the eye.

Wheee! he squeaked going down on his knees and palming his eye.

Dara was next, she took it in the cheek, it split right open. Spinning, Dara's head and shoulders disappeared beneath the crowd.

The bodies in front of me disappeared and the ones behind me pushed me closer to the swinging batons, these flashes of darkness that sent people crawling, touching the hurt parts of their bodies like they'd never felt them before.

The air was full of these things, these flurries of dark through the daylight. They looked strange getting near them, full of energy, and I remember wanting to catch one in the side of my neck—I wanted to crawl too, so that no one could say I hadn't, and then feel myself where the pulse was strongest, feel that skin and that throb again from before anyone else had touched them, thinking, This is mine.

There was nothing to be afraid of. The cameras up in the helicopters were smiling down on me, grinning like old friends, like a dad on a beach somewhere—

"Go ahead, kiddo! Go get 'em!"

The girl in front of me went down screaming, one ponytail flipping up from the middle of her head and over her face. Then I was smiling at a cop, walking toward him.

It was sunny but I didn't feel warm. I didn't feel cold, either—I wasn't inside or outside, I didn't hear a thing.

Tick-tock, I thought.

It hit me without a sound, this fluttering shadow bouncing away from my shoulder. I could have taken another hit, but when it touched me I knew I was supposed to get on my knees, to crawl behind the others, through all those legs still standing.

When we got toward the middle of the column we stood up

again, all of us touching the new parts of our bodies. Dara was holding her sweatshirt to her new cheek, then she took it away, showed me what she'd found, let me kiss her temple just above the gash. I looked Kenny in the face and, without saying anything, he rolled up his sleeve and showed me the purple lump on his forearm. There was a one-two throb beating its way out of my shoulder, so I took off my jacket and flannel, showed them the bruise glowing. We were all being so tender with ourselves, with each other, so interested in all of our new flesh and bone, our muscle and blood.

They'd been right all along, every one of them—we suddenly meant so much.

Except Justin. He didn't want to mean anything, didn't want a new body, so he kept making angel-squeaks and trying to fly. He found a bottle and when it bounced off a shield and he was still standing on the earth he looked for another bottle, turned to us, grabbing at us—rough, frantic. I told him to just keep walking, that we were okay.

He said he'd get them, he squeaked, he tried to fly.

"Damn, Justin," Dara said. "I'm bleeding."

He looked at her, at her bloody cheek—she showed it to him. Then he headed back toward the cops, squeaking to the rest of the angels through his bullhorn.

Wheee! I am a paradigm!

Wheee! I am dominant!

Wheee! You can't subvert me!

I took a look behind me, slipped my arm around Dara's back. Bottles were arcing through the air, they were passing a garbage can over their heads, hand over hand, it was emptying itself on them. Then that was in the air too, trailing burger wrappers, rotting hot dogs, ants, coffee cups, newspaper . . .

"Just keep going," I said. "Look for a space to sneak out of."

I saw a few of the cops aiming their little black canisters, holding them arm's length from their visors.

"Hold your breath."

The air was hot around our eyes, we started crying, gasped the pepper mist. The buildings above us seemed to sway side to side as our eyes ran and we choked on the burning air. All we had to do was let the pain run out of us. It was familiar, we'd felt it before—way, way back. It was the first pain.

3

—

That first shot at college, I stuck with it for as long as Dara stuck with me, but she bailed before my second semester was up. Something kept getting to her—the socialists didn't fix it, school didn't fix it, I didn't fix it, so she went off looking, she disappeared on me.

I started studying the bars of Bell Boulevard. Nothing felt or tasted like much without Dara around, but the strip was always good to watch—it was almost as crazy as she was. Bell had fifteen to twenty bars in the five blocks between Northern and Thirty-ninth Avenue depending on the month, new places opening and closing like movies coming and going from theaters.

As soon as a bar launched the dealers would move in, there'd be a fight—two, three, ten fights—and the community board would start making a stink, move the cops in. Suddenly there's three, four new regulars elbowing you at the bar—a crew of matching buzz-cuts pretending not to know each other, sporting Champion sweatshirts over 'roid-rage arms, the best the 111th had to offer.

"Hey, man," lifting its chin at you, nonchalant, tapping its nose. "You, uh . . . ?"

Businesses dried up in a hurry, new ones took their places, you moved on, and the whole thing would go around again, over and over—it was like TV, like seasons changing. Me, I felt the same in any bar any season, waiting for Dara to come back, scared for her, waiting on Rahmer and Ortiz to finish their time, scared for them, waiting for a new Dara to come around— scared for me.

The only places that lasted on Bell were the ones for money, for normals—sports bars, theme joints, chains—places calling themselves "American" or "Family" with drinks too expensive for the street animals and security guys that crushed balls when anyone except the house dealer tried to pass a gram.

The Irish pubs did all right, too, but I couldn't step foot in them—I wasn't anyone's brother or father, they didn't like my face. Plus, those places were full of the worst kind of cops—the off-duty ones.

I started localing at End Zone, this sports bar on Forty-first and Bell. The drinks cost too much, and I was no friend of the normals, but I knew two of the girls that worked there from high school, Jenny Leibowitz and Carrie Fine—they talked to me, they hooked up my drinks.

The three of us had met back at high school orientation, the summer we were fourteen. Jenny and me had the brother-sister routine going, but Carrie was my first girlfriend—we were drinking my mom's vodka in my bedroom the night the dead kid was asking Rahmer his question.

Nights at Zone, Carrie and Jenny would lock up around four, we'd cut lines right on the bar, seasons kept passing, cops came and went, and the retards' faces blurred, just on the out-skirts of memory . . .

Somewhere in there, Ortiz had gotten out, but he wasn't much good to me—he started choking on his freedom as soon as they served it to him. He had his rights back, most of them, a senator-sized bank account courtesy of Pan Am, and an idea he was going to make something out of himself.

Making something meant going into the city to fuck whores, cozying up to their pimps, their dealers, buying suits, ruining suits, and mostly trying to give the impression to every dime-bag zilch in Manhattan that he had some mystery job during the day—a secret life.

Sure, he had a secret life, but it wasn't the one he tried to play off for those grease-slicked nothings in the city, it was the one that had paid out when he'd turned twenty-one locked down, the one he'd gotten in the Everglades.

He took me with him on his missions sometimes, I couldn't stand it. As soon as the city would rise up over the LIE I could smell the perfume of those girls over at Runway 69 that'd throw a shining thigh over my lap and pull it back again as soon as they figured out that Ortiz was the one with the money.

Anytime I wanted, Ortiz would fix me up, but for every twenty minutes I spent wrestling around in the Private Dance room with some poor thing that ten other guys had just gotten at, I had to put in three, four hours surrounded by Ortiz's new pals—these Tonka-truck mobsters that kept touching you when they talked whether they knew you or not, gold jangling any-where they could hang it.

When Ortiz came by Zone now and then he'd just shoot through it like he was late for a blow job—tapping his fingers on the bar, his silly head going tick-tock with the seconds. Carrie Fine was good to be around, though—we'd been all right to-gether, back a thousand years, just before the shootings and the stabbings, the pipe bombs and everything turning to hell. I'd told her I loved her after a week and she'd shown me her breasts—I was scared shitless.

She always messed with me about it at Zone, leaning right to my ear and whispering, "Run away from me again—I dare you," or "You still love me, don't you?" She was trying to be cool but her glasses would always slip down her nose, she'd start giggling and snorting like some goofy little kid—it felt like we were in front of everything again, back in time, where it could all still come out okay.

Except we weren't, it couldn't.

There were still plenty of retards around and they started acting up every time they caught a look at me. It made their bones itch just to see me walking up Bell with Carrie, getting a pizza, picking up a prescription . . .

Rahmer had always said just to smile at them and they'd pussy up like they always did, but he didn't get that they only did it for him.

The bouncers didn't let retards into Zone but they were out there, in threes and fours, in front of the bars, in back of them, down the side streets—I forgot myself once and went over to Yeats' Tavern with Carrie and Jenny when they had a night off. I remember touching Carrie's wrist at the bar and seeing a flash in my eye—I ducked, a bottle blew up against the wall behind me.

Frankie Venages stood up laughing in one of the back booths.

"Getting some play, Crotch?"

I stood up, Venages's boys stood up—Jenny said, "Retards," shaking her head, and stomped out.

"Sit down," Carrie told Venages. "Stop being a dick, Frankie."

Venages didn't say a thing, sucked his cheek in, head down, checking her through the tops of his eyes. Carrie took her glasses off, slid them in the pocket of her overalls, smiling at him.

"Come here and hit me, loser."

"Nah," dropping his eyes. "Why you want to say that?"

"Come on, Frankie. Show everyone."

"Nah," he was saying, "nah, nah . . ."

"Do it," she said. "Show everyone—I dare you."

I didn't know what I'd do, nothing was coming to me—my wrists hurt, my neck went hot, waiting to figure it out.

I took a step toward Venages, there was a rumble behind me,

glass shattering—something pulled on the back of my jacket, I turned to see it. The bartender was grabbing at me, climbing over the counter.

He said, "Time to go, asshole," and got my arm up behind my back, twisting my wrist.

"Don't touch him!" Carrie screamed and I yelled for her to get back.

Moving toward the door, my arms in the bartender's hands, I could hear them behind me, laughing, one of them screaming, "You're still a punk, Crotch," over another one saying, "Tell your boy Rahmer come see me when he gets out."

Carrie was clawing at the bartender's shoulder, but he wasn't the bartender anymore—he was something I was riding out, he was floating me away from them, getting the door open with his foot and my chest—we were part of the same thing.

The cold hit my face, my neck, and I felt the hands pull me back and push me away, letting go. My own hands barely got in front of me in time to stop the sidewalk coming.

Carrie got down there with me, helped me stand up. We walked up Bell with our arms around each other's backs, stopped at the cab stand and waited.

"I'm sorry I made you go there," she said.

"You didn't make me."

She put her glasses on, the orange streetlights swirling in the lenses, she smiled at me.

"Yes I did."

"Okay, you did."

"You still love me."

I didn't say anything, I didn't have the right kind of nerve. A cab was coming toward us—black dots, pinholes, shivering in the headlights.

The night before I went to meet Rahmer's train from prison Carrie and me went over to Ortiz's and around dawn he was playing us his favorite video.

Rahmer was on the TV in a blurry white room behind a card table holding a can of Sprite with a guy's voice asking him, "So who else did we have on this little adventure?"

Ortiz tapped on his mom's coffee table, laughing, telling Carrie, "Here it comes, here it comes . . ."

That confession tape was all the evidence the state ever had against Ortiz, so the D.A. had had to give a copy to his lawyer, and Ortiz had been hanging on to it as a souvenir ever since— like for kicks. Every time he showed it to me I got the feeling he had a piece of fuselage stashed somewhere, too.

On the screen, Rahmer was sipping the Sprite through a straw, this scrawny kid in a turquoise Ocean Pacific T-shirt with a big curly mop on his head—all beak and neck below the eyes.

"Mr. Rahmer," the detective said. "We both know you weren't foolish enough to leave that little note behind," and Rahmer smiled. "Use your head, my friend."

"Watch my boy crack," Ortiz said, sniffing back the drip, grinning at Rahmer through the side of his face.

"That was Ortiz."

"Served!" hitting the rewind and playing it again, and then again, over and over—

Use your head, my friend . . . That was Ortiz . . . My friend . . . That was Ortiz . . . That was Ortiz—Ortiz, Ortiz, Ortiz.

"On his behalf," Ortiz laughed, passing Carrie the straw.

"What?"

"On his behalf. At my expense."

Scrunching her face at him, Carrie touched the CD case with the lines on it and brushed her teeth with her finger. "Boy," she said, "he sold you out just like that," sucking back the freeze.

"Don't let it get you, schoolgirl—we were kids. And that note was a motherfuck of a bad idea, blew our whole stealth."

Hot behind my eyes, I watched Rahmer's face frozen on the TV, paused in time, wanting to get back in front of it, to stop everything from happening—I slid my fingers up the back of Carrie's head, her hair greasy with Aveda.

The note had said, "Gift for TMR."

"I don't know. I don't know if I'd ever forgive something like that."

"What's forgive? You move, you keep moving—I'm all about that, you move, you go—" He got stuck in the sentence, dropped his eyes—the floor had fallen out of his lift, he grabbed the straw, started trying to bring it back. I cut us a little to-go package from the mound, grabbed our jackets and my book bag from upstairs, and Ortiz didn't even look up when we went out, just hit a button on the CD remote. I could hear his song getting louder and louder as Carrie and me went down his front steps—

Try to set me up for a two-eleven, fuck around and get caught up in a one-eight-seven . . .

The day Ortiz got out I was unloading the industrial dishwasher at the Sizzler on Northern, dying from the steam and my hands burning all over the pots when I hear, "Where's Koch? That ankle-biting son of a whore has a beat-down coming and he'll goddamn report for it today! To-day!"

The kid had come out reborn, to the nines—I'd never seen anything like him. He had on this suit that looked like sealskin, shimmering in the ugly fluorescence, his hair slicked back tight, the sides shaved off, and he'd grown this goatee that made him look like Satan himself.

And the normals, they backed the fuck up. The early birds, the wait staff, that shitheel Chris Tanner that ran the shift—Ortiz made statues out of them, they just stood there not knowing what to do with their idiot faces.

I remember being afraid to run up to him, like I'd go right through him—he'd be mist. I don't even remember taking a step, just Ortiz getting me up in this hug that would kill a pit bull and him saying, "Come here, come here, come here . . ." with his laugh working under it. I was there already, I had my face in his shoulder, but he kept saying to come here, saying come here and lifting me up harder and harder like he was scared I wasn't really there or really me. But I was me—and I'd have never disappeared on him.

Rahmer, though, the first thing out of his mouth is "Get that, get that." He had a shopping bag in each hand and one of them was splitting open, books spinning across the floor of Penn Station—lots of Russians, buckets of philosophy, law . . .

It's possible he stopped and did something to signify the occasion, to say it was cool of me to meet his train when his girl and his own mom wouldn't do it but, you understand, I don't feel like that happened.

We went upstairs from Amtrak to the LIRR, my arms loaded up with his books and Carrie trailing behind, stopped into this Irish place across from the ticket windows, Carrie falling asleep with her head on the bar—we'd been up a day and a half by then.

"She's a trooper," Rahmer said.

"Let me buy you a shot."

When he lifted his head up from the shot I could see it in his face, the mule kick a mouthful of tequila had given him. His head was shaved bald and there was a lot more meat to him than when he'd gone in, but he was shivering, his eyes tearing up pink—there was still something left in his glass.

"Take the medicine."

"Dude," getting a grip on the bar with both hands. "Holy fuck, I'm floating."

"Can't handle it, tough guy?"

He tried to shake it off, looking around like he'd never been in the station before. "It's not just in my head there," he said. "It's the taste. It's like I haven't *tasted* anything in two years—I've got to start getting used to it."

I thought of Dara's sweat like a sting at the tip of my tongue and poured the rest of Rahmer's shot over it. I hadn't seen her in over a year—I was getting used to it.

"Have another," I said.

He shook his head no, asked me to go buy the tickets to Bayside, saying, "I'm not walking around yet. I'm fucking floating."

I told him he was going back alone—my floor had dropped hours ago, we were out of coke, I was almost out of money, and that shot I'd bought him was one less I had for myself, one less against an all-out emergency.

"There's some stuff I have to take care of downtown," I said. "I need to get some money."

"Stuff to take care of? What are you, Ortiz?"

"He wants to see you," waking Carrie up with a tickle to the back of her neck. "We'll all meet up tonight—wherever you want. I'll call you."

"Right. Go take care of business there, tiger."

Carrie was giving me a look, I checked myself for a nosebleed—it was dry.

"What is it, kid?"

"Nothing."

She looked scared, I got an arm around her waist, slow, and slung my book bag over my other shoulder, saying, "You remember Carrie Fine?" Rahmer nodded, gave us the side of his face.

Out in the glare of the station a swarm of flies was arcing into a loop, screaming toward me from the ceiling—I watched the floor, held Carrie tighter, marched us to the subway with my head down.

Carrie knew a guy at NYU we could buy coke from, but she didn't know how we'd pay for it—she'd called in sick to work the last few days, I wasn't working at all, and hitting up Ortiz didn't feel right if he wasn't getting a share in the fun. So I'd gone around my mom's place and gathered up a few valuables to sell.

The guy at the store started Jewing me down before I even finished laying out all the merchandise. The prick starts off trying to give me twenty bucks for an original *Star Wars* hand-blaster—even Carrie knew he was fucking me.

"Let's get out of here," she said. "He's not even for real."

"Dude," tapping the label over the trigger, "that's the original logo right there, that's 1977, not *Empire,* not *Jedi*—this is history you're trying to rape me on, this is Han Solo's."

He scanned us—I knew what Carrie and me looked like, what he was thinking, but I was surprised when he came right out and said it.

"I think you'll take twenty."

"Dude, look—"

"I'm not your dude. You'll take twenty."

"Fuck, Leon."

"Don't curse in my store."

She let out a groan, rolling her eyes, bit down on the sleeve of her jacket.

The walls were covered with all the best things in the world—Boba Fett on the card, a Millennium Falcon with the chess table intact, a twelve-inch Greedo, the Cantina playset with the Snaggletooth in silver boots they'd only sold out of

Sears—and someone had put a hard-ass cunt of a normal in charge of it all.

I could feel it in my wrists, I kept my mouth shut—we needed to finish.

"I'll take twenty."

"Leon!"

"Shh!"

I took out the storm trooper rifle from *Empire,* my throat so dry I didn't know how I'd keep talking.

"Both the settings still work?"

Getting up the last of the air from my solar plexus, I closed my eyes, whispering, "Try it." I heard him playing with it, rapid fire and then a single laser pulse, thinking of all the times I'd tagged Ortiz with that thing.

"Nice. This is another twenty."

"You piece of shit!" Carrie screamed and he pushed the guns away from him, told us to get out.

"Please," I said, "please, please—wait," taking the last piece out of my book bag, Carrie grabbing my wrist, trying to shove it back in.

"Don't," she was saying, "just don't."

"Look at that!"

He was pristine in his box, he was beautiful—his light saber was translucent blue plastic, his boots were beige rubber, he was twelve inches tall and he didn't know yet who his father was.

"Twenty."

"Oh God."

Carrie didn't say a thing, there was no stopping it. We took our money and went to find her dealer.

Later on I was starting to feel all right, we were in Tompkins Square Park sharing a forty of Colt—the kid at the NYU dorms hadn't tried to fuck us, we had hours before I had to meet Rahmer and Ortiz at this bar on Ludlow Street, the sun was slow, going down, it wasn't hot or cold, one of the skaters had Jane's going on his radio—

I am skin and bones, I am pointy nosed—but it motherfucking makes me try . . .

Carrie started shaking and pulling on my jacket.

"What the fuck, Carrie? What?"

She unzipped my jacket and put her arms in it, around my ribs, slid her cheek on mine, but she didn't kiss me—she'd never kiss me.

"When we were with Rahmer and I went to sleep," she said, "I had a dream you died."

"Me?" rubbing my thumb on her neck. "Did someone kill me?"

"I don't know how. But I went to get you and you wouldn't come back with me."

I asked her where she went, she said she didn't know. She asked me if I'd ever had anyone die on me, I said I didn't know.

"There was this girl, this girl Dara," I said. "She just got up and went. She used to write me sometimes, but not even that anymore. So she could be dead—I don't know."

But I told her it seemed sometimes like I might feel it, I might sense something wrong if Dara'd stopped being alive, if she went off for real.

"You won't," Carrie told me. "You wouldn't feel anything. I didn't know it when my dad died—he just died."

My eyes hurt, I closed them but the ache wouldn't go. When I started to rub them Carrie took my hands away and I could feel her fingertips on my eyelids.

"You looked so clean," she was saying, "you looked so clean. You were so clean when I found you—you didn't even recognize me anymore."

I could hear the skaters' wheels, spinning against the asphalt, felt Carrie's palms on my lips.

"I don't want to go see your friends, I don't want to see anybody—something will happen," taking her hands off my face. "Can't we just go home?"

I didn't know whose home she meant, or what we'd do when we got there.

"I want to," I said, "but I can't."

"Something will happen if we go, somebody will get mad and something'll happen." She was breathing into her sleeve, her glasses on the tip of her nose. "We can just go home, we can just go to sleep—it'll just be nice."

"Please, Carrie, please—I want to but I can't."

"Yes you can!" she yelled. "What's wrong with you?"

I didn't know how to tell her, that it was the same with all of them, with her and Dara, with Ortiz, even Rahmer—I went where they wanted me, I had to, and it had to cost something.

I told her, "They're my friends."

I'd put another three semesters in at school when Ortiz put his Eagle into a tree.

He wrecked-out by Queensborough Community College, across the street from the house he was raised in. His mother—you understand, his aunt—had moved to Atlanta with her boyfriend, so Ortiz had sold the house and gotten himself an apartment over in Bay Terrace. I was still living down the end of that block with my mom and stepfather and I didn't know what Ortiz had been doing up my way in the middle of the night but, since he was drunk, the only thing to do was ditch the car in the ravine between P.S. 203 and QCC and report her stolen.

The mouth of the ravine was fifty feet off the avenue, so the streetlights weren't a problem, but cruisers from the 111th rolled in and out of there all night checking for little kids sneaking six-packs and trying to fuck. They were also on the lookout for the jackasses that kept ditching cars in the ravine and reporting them stolen—that was one of Bayside's only traditions. It was a very young town.

The point was, get the fucking thing in the hole and haul ass.

This maniac, though, he gets the tire iron from the trunk, does a key-hit, and smiles at me, says, "You know I'm not passing up such a rare opportunity." Then he's singing, "Brother Can You Spare a Dime?" and smashing all the windows and taillights.

I didn't try to stop him, it was too funny, I laughed until I fell on my knees. Ortiz got down there with me, put his arm around my shoulders and brought the key to my nose.

"I do appreciate that this is not acceptable behavior," he said and, the way we were smiling at each other, I thought he was going to tell me I was right about his mom—that he wanted me to know who she was.

There's this feeling I used to get, this lifting in my chest that made me think I could say anything to someone and they'd take it in a way that would make us better.

That feeling—that was alcohol, that was cocaine.

So when Ortiz got up without saying anything, I thought he was trying to gyp me out of some sacred moment between friends—I believed we could think to each other.

And I thought I saw a cat running under the car before we shoved her in, this flash of black that made me jump, like the pinholes had come together to make a shape.

The next time I saw Ortiz it was a different season.

He showed up at my mom's place in his new Integra, talked me into skipping two finals and going to the track. That kid lost twenty-five hundred dollars right in front of me and shook his head about it.

"What do you want from me?" he said. "Now I've got to know what horses are going to do? You want me to be a god? I'm the god of horses for you now?"

We were pulling up at a light on Francis Lewis Boulevard, these four Indian women passing ahead of us, all done up for a party in red and gold saris—and there was gold on their wrists, gold on their ankles, their long brown hands and feet were painted with bright swirls of red. The sun was all over them. I thought if I put my hands in their hair it would be like burying your hands in the sand at the beach, that kind of warm where you don't have to think—I could kneel down in front of them and stare at the red patterns on their feet and I'd forget who I was.

I thought I was being beautiful.

The last of them, this tiny grandma, was stepping onto the curb when Ortiz eased the car up behind her, reached his hand out the window, and gave her a soft, easy squeeze on the ass.

She learned to fly, went right up out of her sandals. The women screamed as we went away, but Ortiz didn't trouble himself about it, just cruised off casual like he was about to wish top of the morning to someone.

"Are you insane?" I screamed. "Drunk or not—fuck that— are you just an asshole? What kind of person are you?"

Ortiz, he began to sing. He had that smile on his face that made his eyes turn into slits. The tune was "Mack the Knife," but the lyrics were all about the horse god and grabbing ass—he made it up on the spot, snapping his fingers and dancing with just his head. He was charming, he made me laugh.

We had 7-Eleven Big Gulp cups full of ice and Scotch. I was just letting the sun make mine a little more watery—there wasn't any rush, I wasn't going to run out. When I finished it, there was still a brand-new fifth between my boots and if we finished that Ortiz would buy more.

"You hang out at the track," he said, "and there's never anything to remember it by. Even when you win, all you ever remember is was it cold or hot, and that you were surrounded by losers. But I cupped that woman homestyle, kid. That little move shall live in infamy."

I thought our cells were talking to each other, I didn't want to breathe. That was it, though. When we were at the top of the moment, when everything inside of me was begging for Ortiz to tell me who his mother was, he squinted at something that wasn't there, nodded, and dug around for his cigarettes.

And then he disappeared on me again—hard. When he came back around everything out of his mouth was about Boise, this magic city he'd seen on TV, on the other end of the country— opportunity, mountains, new beginnings . . .

Voodoo, tomfoolery—nonsense.

Carrie, Jenny, and me had moved into a two-bedroom off Bell with Jenny's dad cosigning and you could see the city from the top of it—they told me, I couldn't get myself up the fire escape for shit.

The black dots were putting on a whole fucking parade, beaming into me from every corner of the room and me keeping my head still, jaw locked, waiting.

Jenny and Carrie were Indian-style on the floor—twin girl-Buddhas in front of the set, *The Wizard of Oz* glowing at them, *Dark Side of the Moon* trying to keep up in that game that never worked. I was on the futon with Jeanie Riley, Rahmer was out cold on the couch, an arm around Cali holding her knees, her face solid like mine—but perfect, sleek in the blue buzz, eyes wide on nothing—

I thought of an iceberg at night, I held my breath.

Ortiz pulled me up by the back of the neck, I let go Jeanie's hand, he spun me, smirking with his eyes slitting up.

"See much?"

"I'm good."

"It's too bright in here, kid, your eyes can't take it." I started to say something, he put his hand up. "Don't tell me anything—I'm looking right at you."

"It's not too bright."

"Then it's too dark—who burns candles? You're a little fucking hippie, Koch."

"Tell the girls."

Jeanie grinned up from the futon, touched her tongue to her teeth, snapped them at me. There were holes around her face, sucking the candlelight, the blue glow, growing in the dark like pupils.

"Come outside," getting an arm around my shoulders, "catch a breath."

He was pulling the screen up, ducking me, head and shoulders, through the window, and Jeanie giggled.

"Push him off if he doesn't behave."

"You behave, young lady."

The whole building swayed behind the fire escape, it bent me down over the railing, the sidewalk came up to me, I puked over the rail, Ortiz's hand on my neck.

"Feel better much?"

"Oh, absolutely."

"Good news," spinning me onto the metal stairs. "Everyone has to feel better—that's all there is to it." I went to speak and he plucked a finger into the back of my head. "Don't tell me anything—it's in the papers, health's bigger than Jesus, my friend—why can't you get in on it?" I turned my head, he shoved me up a step, saying, "Walk—you're full of shit, that's your whole story—walk."

The roof was two flights up—seven-story building—streetlights blinking orange through the grating under my boots, the whole steel works rattling up through my bones.

Ortiz couldn't be in an elevator without breaking a sweat, but this was fine with him, climbing up into space on a Tinkertoy mousetrap built by men twenty years dead—I had it just the other way around.

Ever since I'd told Ortiz about the spots, he knew when one was opening up at me. Not that he could see them, but he could see me seeing them—every time I was about to freeze he'd press his thumb into the back of my neck, steady me, push me forward.

Up on the roof I saw what there was to see, the boxes of glass lit up like something in a display case.

"Yes?" I said.

"It's a space movie, they should have cars flying around in it."

"That's not news."

"They can smell each other's shit out there," letting go of my neck, lighting a red. "All those people living with their heads up each other's asses—a guy pops his wife in the mouth, it goes in the river, it circles around, it comes right back around for the next fucker that lives there. It never ends, my friend—whatever, two thousand years, ten thousand years—shit."

"Places have nothing to do with it."

"Don't be naive, Koch."

"Okay."

He hissed smoke, flicked a finger across his goatee. "So how's Lazy Eye?"

"I don't know," I said, "I don't give a shit. Out of nowhere she's worried about me? Fuck her."

"Is it working for her?"

"What?"

He leaned his face down, giving shadows to his eyes—I knew what they were doing.

"Don't be a punk."

"How do I know if it's working? You can't believe anything Dara says—she'd call me from a homeless shelter and tell me it's a motherfucking palace."

They'd found her in Washington Square Park one Saturday, found her reading *The Stranger* and zeroed in, these two super-friendly kids, boy and girl, a German and an American—talked her up about loneliness, about fate—

Did she know, for instance, that atonement meant at-one-ment? Atone for what? At one with what?

They brought her to an office on Broadway, smiles all around, there were more of them there—showed her videos, circled her at a conference table, talking and talking, shitting concern and health and love from their drippy eyeballs.

I didn't hear from her for years and then she started writing me from Denver—lots of kids in Denver, needing the love of the Lord.

"So there's no information," Ortiz said.

"Nothing reliable. They could be gang-raping her for all I know and she'd fucking sing to me."

"This tastes like ass," flicking his cigarette out over Bayside. He took the Baggie from his wallet, keyed a hit and offered me the sack. I shook my head at it.

Ortiz tapped the rest of the coke into his palm, scanned me, and blew the mound into the night.

"I've seen that before," I said. "It doesn't mean anything."

"Look. I fly in six hours. What do you want to do with it?"

"Go to sleep."

He went to climb back down and I stopped him.

"Wait," I said.

"What? What do you need?"

"Just stand still." I watched him there with the city behind him. "Just stand still, just don't move."

"Koch—"

"Don't move, don't move."

The city was lit out there, all the windows glowing. I wanted all the lights to go out, I wanted everyone to stay where they were.

He watched me for a second, said, "I can't have this," and got his leg over the edge. He climbed down.

The good-byes were a whole production, the girls jumping up and grabbing Ortiz around the neck, squealing good wishes, optimism, and Rahmer shook his hand, solid, like to be men—I went to my room.

Jeanie crawled into bed with me, started playing with the waistband of my boxers, slid her hand in.

Dara's letters weren't even worth keeping—someone else

could have written any of them, anyone else could've written all
of them—

   You have to find a place to forgive them. I have and I'm
free. Please, Leon. They were only playing their parts. All
of them.

"Leon?" Jeanie whispered.
It could've been anyone talking. Jeanie'd been around eight,
nine months, but that wasn't history—there was nothing to
know her by. And if we ever got the right kind of time between
us, she'd change it, fuck off somewhere to make it cheap.
"Leon, please?"
"Please just leave it alone," I said. "It's dead meat."

4

―

By the time we showed up there was nothing left—no fruits and vegetables, no bread or any meat. We just stared at what was left over, not believing it—the brains of calves, the stomach of a lamb.

We got there after everyone else had come and gone because we'd spent so much time trying to get Carrie to motivate, to get dressed and go out in the storm that was supposed to be the worst in a hundred years. Frankie Venages had come over because Carrie had called him for acid and now she was letting him hang around so she wouldn't have to pay for it—I didn't know if she was letting him fuck her or not.

Venages was with Jenny searching for food in some other aisle and Carrie was with me. She was staring at a jar of tiny fish in oil when this cashier came over, frantic for us to get out.

"You with the glasses," he said to Carrie. "Can't you see?"

"What?" She was squinting at the label—it was in Korean.

"We're closing."

"But I'm still here."

He gave her this look like she didn't belong in the world with him, said again that they were closing, and I told him, "We're going, asshole. Don't make a fucking thing out of it."

We had our faces pointed at each other.

"What?"

"You with the ears," I said. "Can't you fucking hear?"

"I'm just trying to get home," he said.

"Then get the fuck away from me."

"You curse so much," Carrie said when the cashier went away.

"Sorry."

"Can you stop cursing a little please?"

Out the storefront I could see the storm blotting everything out, this white you couldn't see through, the sky the same color as the earth.

Carrie was staring at the fish and I thought I knew what she was thinking, that they came from the ocean and was there anything left in them to see her with?

Jenny and Venages came around with a basket. I remember seeing a bag of Malto Meal in it and no milk. I wasn't interested in their food, it was nonsense, running around the C-Town like a bunch of housewives.

Venages said, "What you got?" and Carrie tightened up, slipped the jar inside her ski jacket. Back in the apartment Venages had tried to put her boots on for her and she'd freaked out, told him to get away from her.

"Damn," he said. "Why you want to be like that?"

"Leave me alone."

He looked at her, shaking his head.

"Nah," he said. "That's not even right."

She told him again to leave her alone and he sucked in his cheek. Then he followed Jenny through the checkout. I stayed behind with Carrie until they had a good lead on us. On the way out I paid for her fish—she still had the jar in her jacket when we got to the door so I went back to the register and paid for it.

"Watch who you treat like a punk," I said to the cashier and he told me again that he just wanted to get home. "Don't fuck ing open your mouth to people and then tell them but you only wanted something."

"Leon!"

Carrie was waiting for me at the exit, she wouldn't go without me—I was her safety. If I'd eaten acid, she'd have been mine too. We had a decade of shit inside of us but we'd known each other before it started, something between us hadn't changed—it's what you wanted from a safety.

The automatic door hissed open behind her, she jumped a little, looked out at the snow and showed me the jar of fish in her jacket.

"Am I stealing this?"

"Nope."

We went out into that screaming whiteness, badly wrapped, holding on to ourselves and keeping our faces down. It was only faith saying that Jenny was up the block somewhere, just a chance that what we thought should be there would be there. From what we could see there was no block, there was only the whiteness.

It was already up to our knees, rushing up and down at the same time, the streetlights turning all of it into this freezing bright haze that was looking into our eyes, our faces, hungry for anything left uncovered.

I spotted the pink glow of the liquor store sign through the snow and started running. I didn't know if it would still be open when I got there or if there'd be anything left in it, but I took off with the hope. I slipped, got up cursing, limped toward the sign, ran swinging my leg out to the side.

"Leon, wait!"

"Ah, fuck."

"Leon, please!"

Carrie was back there in the storm, I'd forgotten all about her. She was standing still, holding on to herself, disappearing in the blizzard.

"Come on," touching her shoulder.

"You were going to leave me out here," shaking her head. "You were going to leave me out here."

"Come on," I said, grabbing her wrist. She didn't want to move, she wanted an apology. There was no time. I pulled her after me by the wrist, dragged her through the lit cold with the sign glowing redder and redder.

"You're going too fast!"

"No time to argue," I said. "This is for real."

The letters were shining, one on top of another, they were climbing down to the street from the top of the night:

WINE SPIRITS

"You're hurting my wrist!"

Jenny was inside waiting for us, the snow melting off the bottoms of her corduroys and spilling onto the floor in the easy yellow warmth that shined on all the bottles, the colored glass. Venages was there, too, and I couldn't believe he hadn't been ditched out in the chaos.

"He practically left me out there," Carrie told Jenny.

"But I went back for you."

Venages said, "That's fucked up, kid—trying to leave her out there."

"Get away from me," Carrie told him.

Venages looked at me but he didn't say anything, just sucked his cheek, taking it. Him and his boys once turned an okay neighborhood into a fucking kill zone, turned kids into meat— and now he wanted to be in love. If he'd had any sense he would've taken his chances with the snow.

I took Carrie's hand, told her I was sorry, and led her past Venages, over to the gin rack.

"Aren't fish trippy?" she said, taking the jar out of her jacket. I looked at it but didn't touch it—it was hers. "Aren't they?"

"Yep. Especially when you're tripping."

"Hey, you," she said, looking up at me through the tops of her glasses. "Tell me they're trippy."

"Oh, absolutely," I said, a black spot buzzing in the corner of my eye. "They're trippy, okay?"

"You don't mean it."

My face was stretched out in Carrie's glasses, curving on the lenses with the colored bottles twisting behind it.

I said, "Sure I do. We'll go scuba diving sometime. We'll bug out on fishes, we'll breathe underwater."

She asked if I really meant it and I said that I did. Then she said that we should really do it sometime, I said, "Yep," and she asked why Jesus freaks put fishes on their cars. I told her it was a secret.

Jenny was leaving, Venages stopped in the door looking at Carrie—he shook his head and went out.

"Really, though," Carrie said, breathing into her sleeve. "What's with the fish?"

"I don't know."

Carrie growled a little, biting the tip of her thumb. "Tell me."

"People carved them on walls before they died."

"For what?"

"To be cool."

I was paying for the liter of Gordon's when I thought of something else. I told Carrie that 666 was Nero's number and that he wasn't coming because he'd already come and gone, and that the world had already ended.

"If the world already ended," she said, "then where are we supposed to be?"

"I don't know," giving the Indian guy a twenty. He smiled at me, he knew me. I smiled back, proud. "Where's your mob?" I asked him. "They cleaned out the supermarket."

"Is this a supermarket?"

We were still smiling at each other, knowing each other.

People whose lives were food went apeshit at the first sign of trouble. Us, though, we were prepared for all things. Our stuff was Armageddon-stocked every day of the year—you couldn't throw us for a loop, the loop was us, we were already thrown. Us, we weren't fucking around.

Carrie was looking around squinting and chewing on her sleeve—something bad had happened and she didn't want anyone to know. I didn't say anything, scanned the store trying to figure it out for her.

Her jar of fish was over by the gin. I touched her elbow, pointing my chin at the jar. She shook her head, poked a finger out of her sleeve, curled it toward her mouth.

"You have to come with me."

"I know."

I walked Carrie back to the jar, she put it in her jacket, I got my change and we went back through the storm together, holding on to ourselves, our faces down.

"It's so much snow," Carrie said, sitting next to Jenny on the couch and taking her boots off.

"Is it freaking you out?" Venages said. He got up from the floor, leaning over her from the arm of the couch. "If it's freaking you out I'm gonna close the shades."

"You're always telling me what you're going to do," Carrie said. "That's why I hate you."

She slipped the cellophane off a pack of cigarettes, slid it back and forth between her fingers.

"You hate me? You just said you hate me?"

I could see it coming into his face, the blood rushing in, the idiot red.

I laughed spitting gin and tonic—there was just the one way anything ever ended, it was funny to me.

"The fuck you laughing at, Crotch?"

"What do you think I'm laughing at?"

That stupid heat—here it was, there it was. I could see Venages watching it in my eyes, then past me—out the window, out in the whiteness.

Jenny pulled her knees to her chest, hugging herself, and Venages stood up.

"Frankie, don't."

"You like to laugh, Crotch?"

"Yep."

"Leon, stop."

He walked past me, opened a window, screaming, "I'll put you in it, bitch!" with the white wind rushing in around him.

Carrie smiled at him and crossed her legs, put her hands on her knee. "Jump," she said. "I dare you."

Jenny was shouting for everything to stop, Venages swung his leg out over the sill and Carrie shook her head at him.

"You hate me, bitch?" He had a leg and a shoulder out the window, grabbing the sill with one hand. "You hate me?"

Carrie nodded, saying, "Look, he's gonna do it."

Venages froze there with the snow catching on his face. I didn't know anymore if he was trying to get out or get in. The snow was swirling in the room, I ducked, covering my eyes.

There was this rumbling through the floor, into the walls, the cold against my skin. I opened my eyes and there was nothing in the window except the whiteness.

Jenny said, "Frankie, stop!" and ran to the kitchen door, stood still talking into the kitchen and I could hear metal rattling in there. Then she was backing away from the door with her palms out in front of her and Venages came out with a steak knife. He looked at Carrie, walking back to the window.

"You always do me wrong," he said, taking off his flannel. "You never do me right."

He pulled his T-shirt over his head, flung it at Carrie—she snatched it from the air screaming, "Don't ever touch me!"

"Nah, I'm not trying to touch you, slut," unbuttoning his jeans. "I'm not trying to touch you."

I stood up in front of Carrie. Venages had his back to the storm in his boxers and socks with the snow blowing around his head, his shoulders, sticking to the hair on his arms.

"Look at me, slut. Look at me!"

She lit a cigarette, laughing. "Look," she said, "he's all naked."

He was so scrawny, the snow clung to his body everywhere, made it bend and twitch like a broken machine. The blade shivered against his wrist and the air turned to mist around his mouth—we were nothing but shapes to him.

If he'd had anything in him, he'd have gone ahead and checked out, but he was a retard, he was a little girl—he dropped to his knees crying, folded up in the white wind, waiting for someone to come help him.

And someone came for him. It was Carrie, she got down there with him—something made her go, the same thing that put Jeanie Riley's hand in an old fucker's rotting teeth. They couldn't help themselves, that thing made them go—I knew what it was, I had it too, I hated it.

Watching Carrie lead Venages into her and Jenny's bedroom, I felt it screaming around inside me and I stared into a black spot, an emptiness—swearing to myself there'd be a way, something I could do, some way to twist my mind so that I'd never feel it again.

If **Venages** could've gotten up the nerve to take himself out of the world with that steak knife he'd have saved the meat-truck guys the trouble of shoveling his body off the LIE in the spring. I didn't know where he'd been coming or going from, I just knew Carrie wouldn't talk to me about it—she'd been asking me to make peace with Venages but I wouldn't even think about it, even when he was dead.

Then she got raped at his wake and she wouldn't talk to me about that either.

The rapist was Stewie Koffman. We used to call him The Littlest Retard because he was the smallest, simplest monkey in the tree. Stewie couldn't fight, couldn't rap to girls, didn't even rank a tag to write on walls. His specialties were smoking dust, dribbling down the front of his Cypress Hill T-shirt, and talking such shit that his own boys used to shove garbage in his mouth.

Stewie was the gang mascot—Venages had given him the position, kept the little douche bag protected, made sure none of his boys went as far as pissing on him when he passed out, even talked girls into fooling around with him here and there.

Then Venages became a thirty-foot smear of chili paste somewhere near the Queens Boulevard exit and Stewie raped Carrie—the girl who'd been in my bedroom, alone with me, the last time I believed I'd grow up to be normal, a human being.

Stewie, he didn't even know he'd raped her. He'd looked so pathetic and lost at the wake that Carrie took him up to Venages's bedroom and mercy-fucked him through the fly of his thirty-dollar slacks. When Stewie began to come he grabbed Carrie around her throat, he screamed out, "Frankie!" and choked her until he was empty.

Carrie would've never told me, she told Jenny and Jenny told me. And I told Rahmer.

Rahmer had been out of prison almost three years but he was still pretty edgy—there was over a year left on his parole, they could've violated him for writing an angry letter. All I asked him to do was drive me over to Stewie's.

We were turning off Bell Boulevard, heading for Oceania Street, where the neighborhood changed. Rahmer was staring out at all the broken houses across the street. He said, "So what's your plan there, tiger?"

"Come on," I said. "What?"

"You want to jump him? All of a sudden you jump people?"

"It's not jumping," I said. "There's no jumping—it's just me."

Rahmer meant that I might as well be five or six people if I was going to beat on a little fuck like Stewie, he meant it made me a punk. I scanned him, he was smiling.

"What?" I said. "What the fuck?"

Rahmer laughed, eased his jeep across the street and into a space across from JHS 158—he'd been class president there.

"I'm not saying anything," he said. "It's just funny. Seeing you all worked up." He wasn't smiling when he said that.

We were around the corner from Stewie's house, it was time for me to get out, but I kept sitting there, I smoked. There was something left that Rahmer was waiting to say, so I waited for it.

He didn't say a goddamn thing.

"All right," I said. "So, whatever."

"Whatever."

Rahmer was an expert on TMR, on punks, on revenge—and he was using it to fuck with me.

"So what?" I said. "The fuck are you telling me?"

"He's going to curl up on the floor, dude. As soon as you fucking touch him. What do you do then?"

We were scanning each other and I was trying to feel strong.

Rahmer had been like that since they let him out—he'd try being your father and being a saint and it pissed me off.

"Whatever," I said. "I'll do whatever I do."

Rahmer nodded, that was it. He tied his hair back with one of Cali's scrunchies, this frilly purple thing. I shook my head, I said, *"Ay, lindo."*

When I was climbing down from the jeep, Rahmer punched the horn and I jumped, fell into the street scraping my palms. Grinning through the window, Rahmer said, "Watch that bitch hands you a beating."

It was spring but it was freezing out, my ears stung from it right away and my eyes started running.

Walking those blocks between Oceania and the Clearview Expressway, I tried to figure out what I'd tell someone if they asked what I was doing there, but I couldn't get a clear thought going. I wasn't going to say I was visiting Stewie, he was a known trash can. I decided I wouldn't answer any questions, just turn around and book if anyone came up to me.

One of the local activists was always in the *Courier* calling those blocks "The Garden of Mixed Lilies." There were some white people living there, but any place with only some whites in it was a black place. I had the choice of walking in their street or walking on their lawns—there weren't any sidewalks, just dirt fading into the asphalt. I chose the street, so no one could get into it with me about stepping on their property.

No one said anything, though—there was no one around to say anything.

I kept thinking about what it would look like, beating up a guy with the body of a twelve-year-old. I concentrated on Carrie, on what could've gone through her head when Stewie screamed her dead boyfriend's name inside her, when he tried to crush her throat with his baby thumbs—that as far as Venages and the rest of them were concerned, she was a thing they could pump themselves into when they felt like it, that since Venages

couldn't use her anymore, Stewie might as well, because someone might as well.

Carrie'd ignored herself to make worms feel good, and one
of them had reached across worlds to say it didn't mean shit. I
thought she might have felt the same when she was a girl and
the cops told her someone had shot her father to death in the
laundry room—they never told her who or why, just that he was
dead.

Stewie's street, this street I was walking on, wasn't a street at
all. A street is black and domed down the middle so that rain-
water flows into the sewer. This thing I was walking on was flat
and gray. They had a sewer though—you could see it right
through the place where the street had collapsed. The hole had
smooth, curved edges, like someone had melted the asphalt
with a blowtorch. Stewie's house was behind the hole—one
story, wood peeling pale green, flat roof—rotting.

I could feel sorry for someone who grew up in a shack like
that. Except I didn't.

Nothing happened when I pressed the button for the door-
bell, so I knocked on the screen door, opened it, knocked on
the peeling wood. It surprised me when a human being answered.

He was medium-sized, my size, maybe sixteen or seventeen,
just a couple dull pimples across his nose and—when he asked
what I wanted—he showed two rows of straight teeth. I knew
Stewie had a little brother, but I'd imagined something else—I
didn't know what to do about him.

"Hey," I said, lifting my chin at him. "Is Stewie around?"

"Who are you?"

"I'm Koch."

He leaned his head back, looking down at me from inside.
"Koch?"

"Yep—what? You know me?"

Now he had this smirk on him and I didn't know what it

meant but I kept my face the way it was—I wasn't giving him anything.

"You're the guy that swam the lake."

I smiled at him, I said, "That's me."

"You're fucking crazy, kid," opening the door.

The stink of the place was onions and old sneakers and something like a wet dog, but I didn't see any food bowls on the floor when we were passing the kitchen. There was a metal garbage can in there, painted orange, with a plaque on it—"Help Keep N.Y. Clean."

Stewie's brother called out for him, coming into the living room, and a noise came from under a comforter on the couch. A woman poked her face out of the comforter. I looked at her and she said, "Is that Richie?"

"No, Mom, it's not Richie—Richie's in the army."

She was checking me out, she had the blood-face—hot red across her nose and the tops of her cheeks, from popping all her vessels, and ghost white everywhere else.

I thought I'd get a face like that, too—all of us would.

Sally Jessy Raphael was on the TV. I looked away from it, at Stewie's mother.

"Richie is a *marine*," she said to me. "You need to get him. You need to *call* him."

George Tatsis had this story that he went over there once when Stewie wasn't home and fucked his mom. He said she'd thought he was Richie. I'd never believed it but there she was, there she was doing it.

She sat herself up, pulling together the front of her robe, and told me, "Richie is six feet tall."

"Okay, Mom," Stewie's brother said, tugging the shoulder of my jacket. I didn't move.

I said, "I know, Mrs. Koffman. Everybody knows Richie."

"You know Richie?" Stewie's brother said.

I knew Richie was their brother, a lot older, and that years ago they'd locked his ass up and he'd deserved it—whole families were like that.

The mother was looking at me like I was disgusting, pressing her chapped lips together. I thought she was getting ready to spit at me. "You don't know Richie," she told me. "You're just a little shit."

"Come on, Mom. Don't be like that."

She had a nasty little bird's face and she was hating me with it. My whole body went hot and started aching everywhere, my pulse jumping up against my skin. She was so angry, her feet were so pretty, she was so small and she hated me so much.

She lay back down under the comforter and I pressed my jacket sleeve to the side of my face to feel the cold coming off it. Her eyes were on the TV, her mouth hanging open, and I followed Stewie's brother into a hall, red and yellow spots bursting all over the darkness.

Stewie was on his knees in front of a black footlocker, breaking up a flat rectangle of pot, his little pink eyes struggling with the stuff like it was math.

"Don't you hear me fucking calling you?" his brother said.

"Shh!"

"Stewie," I said, "you've got guests."

He was looking at me through water. Then he smiled, his teeth twisting out in all directions, black gaps between them.

"Crotch!" he said, getting up. "Holy shit!"

He came over and hugged me. It didn't matter, I could deal with people touching me if I saw them coming—I could make myself not feel it. All I felt was how wet my T-shirt was against my chest.

"This kid swam Oakland Lake," he told his brother, stepping back and holding on to my sleeve, gesturing at me with his other hand like I was something he was showing off. "I thought that water was poison," he said. "I bet five bucks you couldn't do it."

"I know," I said. "You never paid me."

"The fuck I didn't."

"You didn't. You were the only one that didn't pay—everyone in school paid, even Venages paid."

"Venages is dead."

"I know. And you fucked Carrie Fine in his bedroom and you screamed his name like he was your boyfriend."

Everything stopped and there was that second, that second where everyone knows what can happen but nobody knows if they're going to go into it or back away. Then Stewie's brother spoke up, wanting in.

"Dude," he said. "You screamed *his* name?"

"So?"

His brother was laughing at him. "That's fag shit, yo."

Stewie said he was showing respect and that his brother didn't know what it meant to have boys who had your back, what it meant to run with a crew. His brother stepped in front of me, got in Stewie's face.

"I know what fag shit is when I hear it."

The pulse was pounding so hard in me I thought my body would shut down—I needed to get out of there.

Stewie leaned into his brother until they were touching foreheads, both of them up on their toes. Pointing a finger at his brother's temple, Stewie said, "Respect!" spitting.

Then they were down, Stewie curled up on his side with his brother's arm around his neck, swinging his fist into Stewie's face over and over like there was an engine in the hinge of his arm. I didn't care who won, it wasn't my business anymore.

Watching them roll around down there, I felt so angry at Carrie—for trying to be nice to them, for getting raped, for sending me into that house trying to pay something back for her.

I wanted to stop owing.

But I went over and kicked Stewie anyway, because that's what I'd come for. I kicked him in the thigh and then I kicked him again, where I'd meant to, between the legs. It felt like a lot of work.

Stewie's mom squinted at me across the living room. On the TV, a teenage girl was sobbing, doing push-ups with this black giant in army fatigues standing in front of her, barking, his boots almost touching her face—and Sally Jessy Raphael was behind the girl, smiling.

"Is that Richie?" she said.

"It's me."

"Is that you, honey?"

She was lying there and I went and knelt by her head, slid my hands under the comforter, grabbing her sweaty palms and rubbing them with my thumbs.

"It's me," I said and my throat hurt. "You're so pretty. You're so pretty, you're so good but I can't stay."

"Oh, honey," she said, pouting with her white lips and grabbing my thumbs hard. "You can stay with me."

"I can't," I said. I closed my eyes. "I want to but I can't."

I heard a door opening and one of the brothers coming up behind me. Red and yellow spots were blowing up all over her face, I could feel the floor against my knees, my eyes hurt.

"Tell me you love me. Please tell me."

She was crying, the spots went black.

"I love you, I love you—I always love you."

I heard him coming, I didn't move. He came up next to me, we didn't say anything—I touched his mother's cheek where it looked like it was burning and she closed her eyes.

"She's so pretty."

"Everybody says that."

5

———

Sharon Keys was too smart for me and too good and she goddamn knew it, but she took me anyway. She'd been my professor back when I was with Dara, until I dropped out, and when I came back it's like I was an old man if you put me up against the rest of her students. I'd shout them down in class, call them little angels—she got a kick out of it.

By the time she let me kiss her I was already a senior. Her husband was one of these recovering fuck-wits that had always needed a lot of petting but he'd stopped paying it back—that little dope fiend of a yuppie served her right up to me. One night she kept me waiting at the Status Quo for two hours, this bar near her place in Forest Hills, while she finished up some drama with him. All I said when she came into the bar was "Way to show up," and by the time she was done with me I was apologizing for my lack of sympathy.

"I left the girls with him to see you," she said. "You could think about that before you talk."

"I did," I said. "I got angry anyway."

"And when you talk, you could try not to sound like Richard's a houseguest that I left at home. He doesn't have the energy he used to have, fine, he's tired—but he's still my husband."

"I'm sorry."

"I hope you never have to wake up from the kind of nights he's had."

"Please, Sharon, I'm sorry—I just got angry."

"I know." She took a sip of my gin and tonic and waved Daniella over. "I know how dedicated you are to your anger. Bacardi Dark and Diet Coke," she told Daniella, putting down a twenty.

Daniella poured Sharon's drink and walked back to the other end of the bar where these two street animals were playing Quick Draw. She left Sharon's money on the counter.

"What's the little cheerleader's problem?"

"She thinks you're a whore."

Sharon smirked around a plastic stirrer, sipping her rum and Coke through it. "A teenager with severe opinions," she said. "She'll change her mind if you can wait five minutes."

"Not Daniella."

"I remember her from Anarchist Profiles. She's actually very sharp."

"She used to rave about you."

"She should. I'm very good."

"She liked that you wore fishnets to class."

Sharon whispered, "Do you think she wanted to tear them off of me? Do you think she wanted to push me back on my desk and feel my heat against her thigh?"

I kissed her neck, saying, "I think she wanted you to tie her wrists and put her on her knees."

"Oh?"

"You stand over her, you pull her head back. You fuck yourself on her face while she begs you not to. You call her names, you laugh at her—you tell her what a slut she is while you come all over her pretty young face."

"You asshole." She was just loud enough to get everyone

looking over, Daniella and her two skels—a black one and a white one. "You think you can say that to me?"

"What? What?"

Sharon was heading for the door before I even got off my stool, trying to get her coat on. A manila envelope slipped out of the stack under her arm, I crouched to pick it up for her and she pushed my hand away.

"You can't *earn* the right to say that to me."

"Say what? We were having fun."

"Pretty young face," she said. "That's very sharp."

She walked out on Austin Street, I hopped along next to her trying to make my case for half a block. There were all these normals going in and out of the chain stores, they made me watch myself.

I stopped and told Sharon, "You're the best person I know," but she kept going. I ducked back into Status.

Daniella's two trash cans couldn't get enough of laughing at me, the white one holding a Quick Draw card in front of his mouth while the phlegm kicked around in his throat, the black one dipping two fingers in his drink and flicking them in my direction, smiling and nodding like we had a secret between us.

Daniella flashed me a sign with her hand, her index finger and pinky sticking up—"Now who gets the horns?"

The black one started telling me to come over and sit with them, saying, "You come, boy, you come," with some fucked up kind of accent.

"I don't know you."

He stood up next to his stool, he had on black-and-white-checkered cook's pants and a black army jacket, looked practically homeless.

"You know John Gotti?" he said, the white guy reaching up and grabbing his shoulder. "You know John Gotti?"

"Sure."

"That's me. You know General Aidid? That's me. You come, boy, you come."

Aidid pulled his stool back and stood behind me when I sat in it, the white guy asking Daniella for a tequila shot. He poured the tequila into his beer, sucked the top off the mug, and told me, "That's my boilermaker."

"What did you say?" Aidid asked.

"What?"

"To your woman, what did you say to your woman?"

I smiled at Daniella. "I said I wanted to eat her pussy."

Daniella shook her head and the white guy laughed. General Aidid didn't change his face, though, just tapped his nose with his finger, then pointed it at me.

"This woman has very high class."

"She's a whore," Daniella said. "She's married, two daughters—I've seen them."

"If she was a whore, she'd let him at that bush," the white guy said.

"Some whores also have high class," Aidid told him. Then he said to me, "You buy me a drink?" and I shook my head. "I stand up for you, you buy me a drink."

Daniella was already pouring it—vodka and cranberry—so I put down a ten. She took the twenty Sharon had left on the bar.

"She's not a whore," I told Daniella. "She won't let me sleep with her. You know what she tells me? She tells me, 'Then the betrayal would be complete.'"

"Very high class," Aidid said. "I tell you."

I went down to the bathroom. Instead of urinals, Status had an aluminum trough filled with ice. I stood up to it and the white skel showed up in the doorway, fixed himself a key-hit at the sink.

"You want one?"

"No."

"Take one." I was zipping up, he went behind me and held the key under my nose, saying, "You know you want it."

I felt the blast at the back of my throat and his arm coming around my waist.

"This stuff shrinks your dick," he said.

All I did was sniff, trying to speed the drip down my throat. His nails were long and chewed up at the ends, jagged—I could see them working my belt buckle.

"You give me something for the ride?"

"Don't be stupid."

"Just something for the ride, buddy."

It didn't take much to get his hands off me, I barely had to touch his wrists and he backed up to the stall, giggling and rolling his head around like it was just a joke.

"It's always the shitty ones," I said. He had his little Baggie out again, was digging the key into it. "I mean, look at you— you think you can get with me?"

The clear stuff came rolling out of one of his nostrils. He sniffed at it, giggled again, and the drip went right into his mouth.

"I'm just talking about a little nothing," he said, "just a little something for the ride."

"Look at me and look at you—I'm clean," I said, "I'm pretty. You live in a box and you think you're getting some off me?"

When I was walking out, he grabbed my elbow, said, "But you owe me something," so I shoved his hand away, took out a five and gave it to him. We went back upstairs.

Aidid had hit some numbers at Quick Draw, he bought us both a round. The white guy dumped his tequila into his beer and then he didn't touch it, just left the mug on the bar, holding the handle and giving it this hard face.

"Hey, Sala," Aidid said, lifting his chin to him.

"I do the kid a favor and he tells me I'm shit, he tells me I live in a box."

Aidid laughed, reached over and rubbed the back of Sala's neck. "He doesn't know the hotel."

Sala looked over at me with Aidid's hand on his neck, nodding. "Yeah," he said, "he doesn't know shit."

Aidid spun my stool around and put his fist in my face, pressed it hard against the side of my mouth, talking to me down the length of his arm—I didn't know the language, I froze listening, I waited.

"He says go home," Daniella told me.

"But I'm paying."

"You have to go home."

I called Sharon from a pay phone on Austin, her husband put her on.

"If you want a pretty young face," she said, "you can go have one. It hurts me when you say those things."

"I don't want anyone else, I was just talking."

"Don't just talk."

"You don't understand," I said. "These two homeless guys just tried to fuck me."

"Doesn't everyone?"

Up and down the street the last shoppers were getting into their cars, loading bags into their trunks. Their stockings, their jackets, their faces—everything shined in the dusk.

"See me during office hours."

"You don't get it, though, they're not really homeless—they told me."

"Leon."

"You can't find it, the place they go, you have to show up at the right time—sometimes it's not there at all, it disappears."

"We can talk tomorrow."

The shoppers were pulling away from the meters, the dinner crowds pulled in behind them.

"You don't understand, though—"

"My office. Tomorrow."

I'd show up, whether she ever let me touch her below the neck or not, I'd keep showing up, I'd do whatever she wanted— she knew that, she was better than me. Sharon had lived a whole life, she was a grown human being. Me, I hadn't had sex in a year.

Sharon gave me a bracelet and *The Book of Questions* when I turned twenty-four. She sat me in the chair in front of her desk, put the bracelet on me and held the little book behind my head, reading to me in her office.

"*Por qué Cristóbal Colón no pudo descubrir a España?*" she said.

She had her skirt hiked up and her boots on, panties folded on her desk, rubbing herself on my thigh.

"You know I don't speak Spanish."

"You should learn."

She'd never let me see her pussy before—I was fascinated, couldn't take my eyes off it. All the girls I'd been with kept themselves trimmed down to nothing—a little landing strip, tops. Sharon, though, her bush was wild, it reminded me of seventies porn. I moved my hand toward it, she pushed my hand away and I was kind of relieved—it was too dark, there was too much of it.

She lifted herself away from me a little and slipped her fingers into it—I looked at her face and she put her fingers in my mouth. She was unzipping my jeans with one hand and I could hear *The Book of Questions* flipping around behind my ear in the other, her legs tightening around my thigh.

"I want to feel your cock get hard inside me," she whispered.

"Please let me," I said. "We're so close, we're right there."

"We can't, baby, we can't."

"But this is the same thing."

"Let me see a difference if I want to."

"You're a weird girl, Sharon."

"Don't get mean."

"Christ," I said, "I'm not being mean. I'm just wondering why nobody wants to fuck me anymore."

The way Sharon stopped dead, you'd think I'd jammed my thumb into her solar plexus.

"That's not fair," she said.

"I know it's not fair—it's like there's a stink coming off me."

"No, baby, no." She dropped the book and stood up kissing my face, holding it while these little sobs shook her hands. "You know I want to. I want to so much I can feel you in my sleep."

"You could feel me when you're awake if you wanted."

She started crying harder, telling me I had to believe her. I told her to stop crying.

"You want everything at the same time," I said. "You want me to be your boyfriend and you don't want to fuck up your home."

"Then stop seeing me," tucking her face into my neck.

"No."

We didn't say anything, I went to put my junk back in my pants and she grabbed it again, started working herself on my thigh again.

"Don't you ever trim it?"

"You don't like it?"

"I'm just not used to it."

"I think I know what you're used to." She let go of me, she sat still. "Don't compare me to your little girls."

"What little girls?"

"All of those emaciated little playthings your age with their ponytails and their piercings through every conceivable part of their body," looking at me like I was one of them. "When I think of being naked," she said, "when I think of being naked in front of you I think of having to make some awful joke about 'Not too shabby for forty, huh?' You make me so goddamned shy."

"You're crazy," I told her. "You're beautiful. Fuck, Sharon, you've got a fucking engine in your belly—you're a goddess."

Smiling at me out of the corner of her eye, Sharon got up and turned off the lamp on her desk. She leaned back against the desk, we were eyeing each other in the dark.

"What if I don't want to be a goddess?"

"I wish you did."

She laughed coming toward me, got on my leg again, leaned in until our faces were touching—holding my hands against the arms of the chair. "Why do you want me to be a goddess?"

I was trying to think of a way to put it, I didn't have the right kind of nerve.

"To worship," I said. She didn't say anything, turned away like I'd embarrassed her. "I'm sorry," I said and she scanned my face for a while.

"It's dangerous to worship people. Rituals can get old even faster than people do."

She knew a lot, she knew how to put things—I liked that. I was still trying to figure out what I wanted to say when someone knocked on the door.

We froze. There was a shadow behind the frosted window next to the door, its face dark in the glass, making a circle with its hands around its eyes—it couldn't have seen us but I thought it sensed us there.

It knocked again, Sharon covered my mouth with her hand and I kissed her palm.

The shadow knocked again, disappeared from the window, and knocked again. It filled the window again, tapped on the glass, disappeared again, but I could still feel it there with us.

Sharon got off me and sat on the desk, grinning down at me.

"So what is it you wanted to do?"

"Whisper," I said. "He's still out there."

"There's no one out there."

I watched the door, Sharon laughed, hopped off the desk and opened it. "Okay?"

"Let me go down on you."

She shook her head no, locking the door, got back on her desk. "Out of the question."

"You can keep your clothes on, just let me."

"Absolutely not," she said, smirking and pulling up her skirt. I remember crouching between her legs, the way my hands started shaking when I felt her at the tip of my tongue, feeling so in awe of her, so grateful.

I closed my eyes, I imagined being inside of her—we were on a giant white bed together, we couldn't see the ends of it.

My legs started going to sleep after a while, the electric buzz humming down through the muscles, making them twitch, and I didn't know where my cock was in the dark—it felt alive but far away, its pulse dying in space.

I heard her breath up there, catching in her throat, and felt her hand on my head—her thumb and pinky pressing into my temples, her palm pushing my head back as she brought herself forward against my face.

Her calves pressed into the backs of her thighs—my arms were between them, locked between them. She pushed my head back farther, her hair was everywhere, she was everywhere—my chin, my nose, I thought she'd come in my eyes.

I twisted my face away, trying to talk. It wasn't easy to get the words out, I had to break Sharon's rhythm, but I managed.

"Tell me to worship you."

"I don't like that."

"Say it."

"Worship me."

"Tell me to pray to you."

"Stop that."

"Say it—stop being such a pussy."

"Pray to me."

"More."

"Pray to me . . . Pray to me you slut . . . Pray to me you fucking slut."

I didn't make her speak again, she'd said enough—I played it on a loop in my head trying to get her off. The back of my neck started to burn and there was that ache in the hinge of my jaw—the place she wanted my tongue to reach could've been in Sirius.

Now and then I'd picture some little goth girl from wherever, picture Sharon doing this to her.

She stopped against my mouth, shivered, then went rigid. I opened my eyes. Her fingers slid away from my face. She said something, it was caught up in her breath, I couldn't make it out, I waited.

"Make love to me."

"Really?"

"Hurry."

The floor shifted and my legs screamed standing up. I dropped my pants around my ankles, watching Sharon's face, and had an idea it was a last look.

She whispered for me to come closer, said, "Kiss me." I was shaking, she slid me inside of her, I closed my eyes. "Don't go away on me," she said. "Look at me, baby, look at me."

Sharon was smiling at me the way you'd smile at a kid showing you a handful of sand. It was so quiet I felt like we were a statue standing there, and I swear I heard the knock before that madman's fist ever touched the door.

Sharon said, "Oh fuck!" and there he was in the window—this shadow, this shape. She was whispering for me to stop.

"Absolutely not," holding her tight around her ass.

"He can hear us."

That was good news. I wanted him to go back to his people and tell them all about it, tell them there'd been a miracle on the other side of the door.

Once I got it back, it didn't belong to Sharon anymore. She was right about the little girls, the starvings, the freaks—I wanted them, there was no deprogramming it.

She'd given me a picture of herself in college, puny and shy, hands behind her back, head down in front of the Grand Canyon or something scary important like that, barely looking at the camera, just through the tops of her eyes. She had on a Velvet Underground T-shirt, dirty jeans, combats—I'd gotten to her twenty years too late.

"Look," I said, "just trim it, just do something."

"Go to hell, Leon."

I could hear Carrie and Jenny fighting in the living room, and the TV droning—

"Now. More than ever."

"Okay," I said, "don't—that's how your husband likes it, all wild, all natural—fine. I want to keep him happy."

"You asshole," slipping on her panties.

She was going around the room in a hurry, snatching up her socks, her slacks, getting it all on in a hot little frenzy. I didn't give a fuck, I felt ripped off—she could give me devil eyes on the quad for flirting with a girl my age and she could go home and fuck her husband at the same time—she could have her whole life, plus me in between, me eyes-deep in museum-style bush.

"It has nothing to do with my husband," she said. She was stepping into her shoes—if she'd had any idea, she'd have told me to kiss them, God knows I tried to teach her, but she wasn't into sickness.

She'd gone to Central America to meddle in someone's elections, she'd visited coal miners, sharecroppers, helping them get their heads kicked in for unions, medical coverage, Ping-Pong balls . . .

"Your whole generation has a phobia about the vagina."

"Oh, darling, it's not just that."

"You're afraid of maturity, of sex itself—the human form, nature itself."

"Maybe it's just you."

"Oh, honey, you don't even know."

"But you still want me to eat your pussy."

"Don't do me any favors."

I didn't want to be funny or nice about it, I wanted her to go back to her husband, to the adults, and let me get to wherever it was I'd been heading all along. Sharon was a great teacher but what she taught was for normals, for humans, and everything in me still said that in the history of the world you couldn't find enough of them with their heads out of their asses to fill a city bus.

They just weren't for me— I wouldn't let them school me into their tribe, teach me their ways.

Sharon left and I imagined some other type being out there, someone perfect, from the same tribe as me—that our DNA was making us ready for each other, spinning us into the same circle, closer and closer all the time. I thought the first part of my life was over.

6

—

We met up in Miami after I graduated and it took Ortiz four days to decide he's going to marry this stripper Rosanna and take her back to Idaho with him.

He was buying dresses for her and one of her girlfriends came along with us. I'd had sex with this girl, Rosanna's friend, and I was willing to buy her things if it made either of us feel any better, but we didn't kid each other about anything. I didn't even talk to her, since it only seemed to make her hate me more.

Outside of this dress shop, Ortiz started checking out greeting cards in a rack on the sidewalk. He had Rosanna on one arm and shopping bags in his free hand and suddenly his face broke up, he was crying. I could see his shoulders shaking as he turned away from me and the shopping bags dropped, spilled over on the sidewalk. It couldn't have taken but a second for me to get over to him—Rosanna, poor girl, was on the sidewalk grabbing up her dresses—but Ortiz was already laughing when I touched his shoulder.

"I'm such a pussy," he said, with that smile, with his cheeks still wet and his eyes gone pink. He nodded at the card rack, smirking—they were Mother's Day cards.

"So I get choked up," he said. "I mean, come on." I scanned him, waiting for him to say it. He said, "Now let's get a drink."

I did twenty-eight shots of some kind of murderer 'cane liquor in thirty minutes, set a record at this shitty little tiki bar, and got so angry my wrists ached. Ortiz slapped me on the back, I saw a cat, and ducked covering my eyes. When Ortiz got me to my feet, I punched him in the mouth.

He was holding on to his face, blood-dots dancing down the front of this gorgeous silk cabana shirt that changed colors depending on the light—all of them were ocean colors.

I woke up puking in the hotel with Ortiz flapping his busted lips about Rosanna—she was gone, so was his wallet. I told him he was a fat fuck, I told him, "Find that whore yourself" and checked out while he was off trying to track the girl down.

I went to the airport, got my ticket changed, and flew back to New York without even leaving a note.

It didn't take long to patch things up—crack some drunk fuck in his face and he'll still need someone to call next time he's home alone.

Back in Idaho, Ortiz moved this Hooters girl in with him and she ditched a month later. She'd found him in his boxers in the back seat of his car with all his clothing in the front seat—he'd apparently used a very good suit trying to mop up the liter of gin he'd smashed between his chest and the steering wheel when he'd crashed into the side of the garage.

"But you're okay?" I said. "Flesh and bone?"

"Stuck the landing, my friend. Iron and steel, kid, iron and steel."

I listened to his ice cubes whispering in the receiver, took a sip of my own.

"You are a giant."

Jenny fell asleep with all her candles burning and when you threw in the damage from the hoses there wasn't anything left you could call an apartment.

The thing that pissed me off wasn't losing the apartment, it was all those fucking firemen, smirking at us through their gay mustaches, us huddling up on the sidewalk—like infants, fidgeting around in our underwear, in the middle of the night.

If I'd had the nerve, I'd have shoved Jenny out of my life with both hands and feet—she'd brought the authorities into our circle, right into the place we lived, had us standing around answering questions from strangers.

I couldn't even get myself to yell at her, though—I'd known her too long, she was too sad, but I told her I was getting a place of my own. Carrie'd had enough, too. She packed herself off to some rehab farm upstate—her dad's life insurance paid for it.

Jenny moved in with some girls from the bar she was working at and I found myself a studio in Kew Gardens, rent stabilized at $652 a month. And I found a job, and then another job, and a few more after that.

The girls were gone, Ortiz was gone, Dara had the Lord, Rahmer and Cali had each other, off on some trip of their own, Sharon had the human race again . . .

I had XxTiggerFan20xX, a femme lesbian preppy sub on America Online, into Winnie-the-Pooh, Sarah McLachlan, and getting slapped in the face by vampire girls.

Her real name was Kristen, she was legal, but not *too,* a terrible little brat—the quote in her on-line profile was "No, you have it backwards. It is better to live on your feet than to die on your knees," from *Catch-22.*

That quote had all sorts of literary boys instant-messaging Kristen every five seconds, each one of them sure as their lives that he was that special guy who'd get her straight if she'd just hear him out—how smart he was, how sensitive. I usually ignored those dudes when their I.M.s popped up on my screen. Or sometimes I'd send them a simple "Ewww!"

Rituals can get old even faster than people do—I heard Sharon saying that a lot, two or three in the morning, with Kristen begging for the same things over and over until I could type it all left-handed.

Inventing Kristen's screen name was a natural—all the sub girls named themselves after Disney, after toys and fairy tales. Her real name took a little more time. If it hadn't been Kristen it would've been Ashley, which was pretty much the same thing.

And it worked out nicely for a while, going out there bodiless to get off without really meaning it, making friends that weren't friends, having sex without touching anyone—with no one touching me. It was fake, easy, it was nothing, but, you understand, it didn't cost a thing.

The Pakistani kid at the 7-Eleven had been riding my ass for months when we finally had it out.

"Okay, stop," I told him. "Stop shaking your fucking head at me, stop rolling your fucking eyes at me."

"Fuck?" he said. "You want to say *fuck* to me?" He started climbing over the counter and the manager, this Chinese guy, was pulling him back by the shoulders. "You want to fuck me?" the kid said. "You want to fuck me, you drunk fuck?"

It was about eleven at night, my workday had just ended, his was only getting started—we'd both had enough of each other.

"Don't touch me," he was telling the manager and the both of them started yapping away at each other while I stood there putting my dinner in a bag—four microwaved White Castle cheeseburgers. The Chinese guy was waving his hands in the kid's face and the kid was pointing at me, saying, "You saw him, you saw what he said! This is bullshit!"

"You're bullshit," I said, walking off with my bag. "You've got an attitude problem and you fucking know it, asshole."

Again, the kid tried to jump the counter and the manager pulled him back. He had some spirit, more than I'd given him credit for, and I realized I didn't really want a fight after all. So I went home.

My problem with the kid was that he couldn't keep his ideas to himself. Sometimes I'd drop something on my way to the register or stumble a little, maybe put down a five thinking it was a ten or whatever, and the kid would shake his head at me and smirk. He thought I had no business purchasing food, having dinner. He never said anything but I'd ask for a pack of reds and he'd stare at me for a second before he'd bother reaching for it. Or he'd leave my White Castles sitting there on the counter steaming in their wrappers and I'd have to ask him to put them in a bag for me like he'd have done automatically for anyone else. And then he'd give me that fucking smirk.

You get back from work and some little angel flashes you this tight, disapproving face like all of a sudden you're his dad or his son—it was too cheap.

The whole day had been for shit—Ken Friedman had ordered me into his office for going off script on a cold call and all the other schedulers could see me taking a beating through the glass, Friedman leaning over me in the chair and me just nodding my head, just taking it.

Every couple of weeks a new script would come down, the new Bible, and the lifers would crush your balls if you ignored it.

"How do you expect us to know if our marketing works when you're going off book?" Friedman said. "How do we know what our research is worth?"

"I couldn't tell you."

"No you couldn't, could you?" He came around his desk, stood at my elbow with his hands on his belt, looking down at me—posing. I just kept my eyes on his empty chair, his pale green sport jacket draped over the back of it.

I said, "No I couldn't, Ken."

"Then let me ask you something you do know. Who is not the boss?" I kept my mouth shut, he said it again—"Who is not the boss?"

"I couldn't tell you."

I could feel everyone at my back, the whole office, watching this happen through the glass wall. This girl I had lunch with once, this actress, she was out there too, seeing me take it.

Friedman got in front of me, leaned back on his desk and his pant legs hiked up over his socks. "Well I know I'm not not the boss," he told me. There were these pink and red splotches flaking on his shins like dozens of cigarette burns. "I can't not be the boss," he said, "being that I am the boss. So who's not?"

"I'm not."

"Who's not?"

"Come on," I said. "Come on, Ken."

"Look at me."

There were the chapped lips, the runny eyes, and the Hair System shifting on top of his head when he smiled.

"I'm not."

The law at the Men's Hair Club was that we didn't sell wigs or toupees, we sold Hair Systems. All the lifers had them, these rugs sewn into what was left of their natural hair and glued onto their scalps. The idea was that if you told a sucker he should go check out the latest Hair System he'd think there was some kind of magic in it, he'd ask what a System was and you'd tell him that it couldn't be explained, it had to be experienced—you had to get them by the imagination. Friedman had experienced the fuck out of it, I was trying not to look.

"Are you sure you understand?" he said.

"Yes," I told him. "I'm not the boss."

"And what am I?"

"This is weird."

"What am I?"

Something was too happy in that peeling smile of his, the dribbling eyes. The way Friedman was looking at me I started thinking he was going to tell me to suck his dick.

I looked him in the face, I did the whole thing just like he wanted, saying, "You're the boss."

It didn't feel like it mattered anymore, some old nut rotting in the mouth catching a hard-on at my expense. I wasn't angry at it, it was just traffic, the weather—but then Friedman made me say it again, that he was the boss, and he grinned at me again, the System shifted again, and I felt myself starting to shake.

The sides were combed forward and the front was puffed up to hide fabric holding it all together, the matrix. It was so desperate, it offended me.

Friedman was asking me if I had a marketing degree and I could feel the tremble coming up through my skin.

"No," I said.

"Are you sure? Are you sure you don't have a degree in marketing you're forgetting about?"

I laughed, telling him, "I get it."

"You get what?"

"I don't think you're exactly a homo," I said. "You're more like one of these secret S-and-M dudes that doesn't care who he plays with."

I waited for Friedman to say something, but he just got this serious face on and started nodding his head, like he was very interested in hearing what I had to say. He put his hands in his pockets and I watched to see if either of them started moving.

"Am I right?" I said. "I mean, why are your hands in your pockets?"

His light blue collar was dark around the edges, wilting with sweat, his skin sagged at his throat.

"You know, Andre wanted to lay you off in the last round and I stood up for you—I've always stood up for you."

"Thanks."

He nodded again, grinned at me, saying, "You're just a regular badass, hey, Koch?"

"Why are your hands in your pockets?"

He looked down his body. "They're there," he said, "because I want them there."

"Why, though?"

His slacks were loose enough that I couldn't make anything out. Friedman scanned me for a second, then showed me his hands—turning them over, slowly, like there was some sign of innocence painted on his palms.

"I quit."

Standing away from his desk, stepping to me, Friedman crossed his arms on his chest and sucked his lips into his mouth. His lips were wet, he said, "You don't have to quit."

"I don't have to suck dick, either."

He folded up laughing, the System doing a panic on his head. "Where in the world do you get this stuff?"

"I don't deserve this," I said. "I work leads from last Christmas, I raise the fucking dead out there."

"Just stay on the script, okay?"

The whole thing had cost me half an hour and I was pissed about it. I was surrounded by abandoned cubicles out there—dead phones, empty headsets, Hair Club calendars still turned to last month.

Ortiz had given me a flask as a graduation present, inscribed, "Wherever you go, there you are," from *Buckaroo Banzai*. I took a sip, gagged on the warmth of the gin, sipped again, and put on my headset.

"Do not call!" was written on the index card for James Tyson of Alabama, next to Katie MacIntosh's initials—they'd fired Katie two months ago. I punched up the directions to the Birmingham office and gave Tyson a ring.

"Praise the Lord," a woman answered.

"Hey, hello," I said. "Is this Mrs. Tyson?"

She was scared already, you could hear it—only the very old wanted phone calls from strangers, and we shit-canned their cards as soon as we figured out who they were.

"This is Leon from the MHC," I said. "I'm returning Mr. Tyson's call."

"The MHC?" She didn't say anything for a few seconds, then she said, "Oh for God's sake—are you those hair people again?"

"Well, fuck yes!" I said, taking a hit. "When's your old man coming to see us?"

"What is that you said to me?"

"Just imagine," I said over her, "a full head of hair to grab on to while big Jimmy's getting a nose up in your gash."

I must have gone through another six, seven calls before one of the lifers listened in. I remember telling this guy on Lake Shore Drive that I wanted a girl shaped like a duck.

"You know," I was telling him, "like with a little belly and her ass kind of curving up—like there should be feathers sticking out of it."

Friedman and Andre Bennet were coming at me across the room, Bennet in the lead, Friedman trailing behind with a smile on his face.

"Hello, ladies."

"Get out," Bennet said, his body rumbling down my aisle, shaking the window frames. "I will physically remove you."

The man was all business, gray suit and everything—from upstairs, the sixteenth floor, marketing—with a System black as an eight ball.

"Of course, of course." I took the mouthpiece off my headset, went to put it in my book bag, stopped, tossed it in the garbage.

"I will physically remove you," Bennet said again, stepping into my cubicle. Heads and shoulders started popping up around the office, over the beige dividers. The actress, she was there too.

"They haven't gotten you yet? Well don't worry," I told her, "you're beautiful." She squinted like she had a question, tilted her head sideways, and ducked back into her cube.

By the time the late-night E goes local in Queens there are almost no whites on it at all. There were black folks, Mexicans, Indians and Pakis, Chinese, Puerto Ricans and Dominicans, Khmers, Pinoys . . .

This guy laughed at me across the aisle and I noticed a cigarette burn through the crotch of my slacks. I put my jacket over it and went to sleep.

7

Carrie might have been out of rehab a month when she started partying again. It was Christmastime, she was all giggly with the spirit when she called saying her and Jenny were coming over.

"I've got work in the morning," I said.

"So? It'll just be nice, it won't be any craziness."

"And I believe you."

"Come on, Leon," she sang. "I'll let you play with my hands."

Carrie came over with this tiny Christmas tree and Jenny was carrying—she cut the lines on one of my CD cases while Carrie set the tree up with candy canes, tinsel and glass balls, the whole thing. I told them that I didn't do coke anymore, that I had to teach class in the morning, but they looked like they were having such a good time.

We hit our old stride right away, drinking and chatting each other up as fast as we could, touching each other when we spoke, telling all the old stories, Carrie rewinding "Velouria" over and over until my machine ate the cassette.

Late, with the night almost gone, I sucked Carrie's fingers, read her palm for her, Jenny's too—Carrie would live by the ocean, Jenny would catch the clap. Jenny grabbed my arm, pulled away blood, Carrie laughing, saying we were in love—I said it was true, to both of them, and started to black out.

It was all three of us on the futon, I curled up under the comforter, mumbling for them to save me a line or two, just something to ride to work on. The futon was good if you knew how to be a corpse, let yourself curve into the deep sag of the cushion, let all your weight settle along your spine, wait . . .

The lines were there when I woke up, four of them under a glass bowl on the coffee table. I reached back over Jenny's head and slapped off the alarm, trying to sit up, got too dizzy and fell back again. Then there was this shape, this darkness moving over my body on the comforter in the weird blue light.

"Why would you bring a cat in here?" I said.

Jenny didn't answer, neither did Carrie, and after a few seconds I realized I was hallucinating. It was cool, though, watching the thing walk over my stomach, her shoulders rolling forward slow and smooth until she sat herself on my chest. She had no weight but she was solid enough that I couldn't see through her.

"Okay," I said, "disappear now," but the cat just stayed where she was, like she was proving a point. My head was so light, I couldn't feel my body at all, and I tried to make the cat into something else, squinting at her to twist her shape, but she wasn't having it.

It could have been a full minute before the color of the morning started coming through the cat and hollowing her out. I said, "That's progress," and lay there with my body coming back to me as the room brightened up.

I felt Jenny's thigh under the comforter, against the backs of my fingers. We'd been brother-sister for years, and her leg was hairier than it needed to be, but I sprung one anyway. I let it be for a while, like a flashback to a healthier year, then I rolled off the futon and, standing up, felt my stomach twisting in on itself and ran to the bathroom.

Ortiz called it vomiting backward. On the phone one night he'd said he thought he'd get so sick of the stink of his own shit someday that he'd start puking every time he hit the bowl— I'd estimated the condition would take him out in three to four weeks.

"You're no doctor," he'd said.

"I don't need a license to practice medicine, boy."

"Boy? I will slap you like my son—wait for it."

"I'm right here," I said. "I'm waiting."

From the bathroom door I saw that the Christmas tree had gone over, there were shards of colored glass all over the carpet by the wall and tinsel clinging to the wallpaper, but the girls looked so perfect sleeping there.

Carrie's knee was shining out from under the comforter, Jenny was all tucked in, but it was no problem making out the shape of her ass. They were such perfect girls, I wanted them to stay, everything forgiven—they could have whatever they wanted, just so long as they stayed and I could hear them talking at night, hear their voices.

Quiet, careful, I put the bowl aside, did a line and got dressed. I scooped the other three lines into a dollar bill, folded it up, and left a note under the bowl—

Hey, angels, you want to have dinner when I get back?

They'd loved making dinners, Jenny inventing drinks and giving me key-hits while I chopped garlic, Carrie funneling out the inside of a loaf of Italian bread, rolling it into little balls that would turn to mold in the corners of the room.

I went to work dreaming.

I wasn't much of a teacher, but the Learning Institute of New

York wasn't much of a school. Legally, the place didn't exist, it paid no taxes, was accredited by no one. They paid cash, though.

I had three classes a day Saturdays and Sundays, prepping third, sixth, and ninth graders for the citywides in English. There was no telling if the kids were learning anything, I ran out of materials after the first month, and, still, the director never said a word to me. From the beginning I'd been expecting to show up and find the place gone, all the signs removed and another business in its place—like what happened to massage parlors. That was Flushing, shops terraced one on top of another in jagged little pyramids, whorehouses in office spaces across the hall from travel agencies and immigration lawyers—everything a secret.

My third graders were screaming when I came into the room. There were twenty-six of them packed into a converted office with a flimsy blackboard tacked to one wall and the first row of desks coming right up to my legs.

They were all looking toward the back of the room, shrieking and passing things to one another. The floor seemed to be slanting under my feet, I was getting dizzy, but I could make out a sentence or two in the chaos—

"Give it here, yo!"

"Man, lemme get some of that!"

All those little fists moving, sneakers pounding the legs of their chairs, the screeching—it made the blackboard rattle against the wall.

"Yo, Bonkers," one of them screamed, "lemme get some."

"Bonkers!" I yelled. "Bonkers!"

Bonkers was Benjamin Su, this dough-faced kid with his hair standing on top of his head and eyes puffed up like he hadn't slept in three days, always working his way through some monster Slurpee or a thirty-two-ounce Poland Spring bottle full of orange Hi-C.

Not one kid even turned around to look at me, so I pulled a Captain Quint on them, riding my fingernails down the blackboard until they all screeched grabbing their ears.

After a second, Bonkers looked at me and said, "What the fuck, yo?" and the room exploded, all the kids shrieking and pounding their desks.

He had a shopping bag on his desk, spilling over with mini Snickers bars, loose sticks of Twizzlers, Juicy Fruit, boxes of Nerds, Blow Pops—all over the desk, on his lap, spread out around his feet like a piñata had gotten an enema. Half the kids had candy sticking out of their mouths, their cheeks smudged brown and red.

"What the hell do you think you're doing?"

"Dude," he said, "it's my birthday and shit."

I had to force myself to speak, the lift I'd ridden to work was already sinking, down into my solar plexus, where the wind was.

"Well happy birthday," I said. "Now put everything back in the bag and don't let me see it again."

"But it's my birthday," not lifting a hand to put away his candy. The kids did a lot of that, saying things that didn't have to mean anything but would take on so much by the time it crossed the room. Like, maybe this was the closest thing to a birthday party Bonkers was going to get, and maybe everyone knew it. That hair standing up, the sleepless eyes—I couldn't stop myself thinking what could go on in the kid's house, in all their houses.

They were all staring out at me, frozen with their candy in their mouths or in their hands, some of it still in wrappers, waiting on their desks. Bonkers was chewing the collar of his Dragon Ball Z T-shirt.

"I'll be right back," breaking a fresh, itching sweat and heading for the bathroom. Unfolding my dollar bill in the stall, digging the tip of the key into the mound, it could have been the Declaration of Independence, I was so careful, so afraid. The lift rose up in my chest the second the blast hit the back of my throat—the taste was a promise.

I heard a scream as soon as I stepped out of the bathroom, a howl tearing through the walls, and I ran.

Bonkers was in the aisle in some kind of kung fu stance, his fists upside down at his waist and his knees bent, feet shoulder width apart, screaming at the top of his lungs.

"Bonkers!" I said. "Bonkers!"

He wasn't saying anything, just letting out a steady scream, stopping to get a breath and then starting over. The rest of the class watched him with their mouths open and nothing coming out.

"Bonkers! Bonkers!"

He screamed again, face trembling, eyes closed—I figured he'd finally gone insane, that he'd decided to let himself, he was tired of playing.

Dr. Kwan came in.

"What is this?" he said and Bonkers let out another one. "Benjamin, stop that! Stop that right now!"

Bonkers let loose again and it seemed to me that he didn't have to stop if he didn't want to, that he'd discovered a way out—he'd made up his mind.

"Benjamin!" Dr. Kwan said again and the little bastard clammed right up, smiled at Dr. Kwan, telling him, "Birthday screams."

Dr. Kwan told him to take his seat, that his parents would get a phone call, that he needed to get serious or he'd end up eating out of garbage cans someday. Bonkers rolled his head.

"Control your students," Dr. Kwan told me.

The sixth graders came in next, I paid two more visits to the stall, and then there was lunch. I called my place from a pay phone on Main Street to check in with the girls.

"Hey, it's me," I told the machine. "Pick up the phone."

"Leon's not here," Carrie said.

"It's me, it's Koch."

"Oh," she said. "Hey, why did you take all our coke?"

"Why'd I do your what?"

"We saved some and it's all gone now."

"Ah, fuck," I said, opening my jacket to let the cold air in. "I'm sorry."

"That's our fucking coke, Leon."

"Look, I'm sorry—it was an accident, I'll bring it back."

"But we don't have it."

I started unbuttoning my shirt and pulling it out of my pants, letting the air hit my chest and my stomach.

"I'll be back in two hours."

"Really, Leon—fuck you."

Back in the bathroom, I snorted the last of their coke, licked the bill clean, and went out to teach the ninth graders.

Amber Ling was cuffing her twin sister's jeans for her and her sister was drawing a face on one of the knees. Linus Ng was sliding his fingers over Sue Yeung's hair—she'd just gotten it put into cornrows. Sonny Maodza leaned over to Crystal Chen, whispering in her ear, Crystal wincing and putting her hand in his face, saying, "Don't touch me!"

She grabbed Sonny's wrist, pushed his hand away from her.

He said, "No one's trying to touch you, skank."

"You wish."

Sonny said Crystal had fucked some kid named Roger, Crystal said Sonny's sister had caught him sniffing her panties in the laundry room, and the class blew up.

"Ewww!"

"What the fuck, kid?"

"Damn, your sister? Shit's *ill*."

Sonny couldn't deny it hard enough but it didn't matter what he said—it was too good. Crystal had him fucked.

Sniffing back a drip, I said, "Everybody shut the fuck up now."

They stared at me, tilting their heads. "Damn," someone said.

In the middle of the room, Vivian Chow took a piece of gum out of her mouth and handed it to Jenny Li-Cheuk. Jenny chewed it for a few seconds, passed it on to James Su, the three of them giggling, shaking in their chairs.

They all started laughing again, they kept getting louder, I kept sniffing, trying to taste just enough to keep the floor from dropping out. I tasted blood, went out for air, and called my apartment again.

"Jenny's sick," Carrie said. "I have to drive her home."

"But you don't drive." I pulled my shirt open, gulped the cold air. "You can't drive."

"Well what do you want me to do? She puked all blue, Leon. Like she puked all this blue water."

"Ah, fuck," I said. "That's coke—don't you know what that is?"

This guy in a white uniform was hosing down the sidewalk in front of the East River Restaurant, I thought I'd ask him to turn the water on me, that I'd let my clothing freeze to my skin.

"Well she wants to go home," Carrie said.

"Call a cab."

"I'm not calling any cab."

"Call a doctor, call fucking nine-one-one, Carrie—this is serious!"

"Don't yell at me!"

I said, "Use your fucking head, bitch!" but I was talking to a dial tone.

This waiter we had, he'd been old long enough.

"Look at him go," Livia said.

It's like he was crossing the desert, with that tray and our drinks, heavy on his legs and shivering—I thought I wouldn't do a lot better if someone expected me to carry much of anything. He shook setting Livia's drink on the table, the pink dribbling down his wrist from the rim of the martini glass.

She took a sip, scanned his face smiling and said, "I'm not marrying your son, am I?"

He cocked his head sideways, his eyes were as deep in his skull as you could put them. "What's that?"

"I'm not marrying your son, so why don't you take this back and put some liquor in it?"

"You order a kiddie drink," he said, "so there's your kiddie drink."

Livia said, "Whatever," her bangs shifting across her forehead, black streaked with red. I wanted to laugh but I kept my mouth shut—I was supposed to be her slave. This was an audition, our first date. She'd already been through three slaves—before that she was a sub like the rest of us.

We'd met in this D&S chatroom on AOL. She wasn't in any rush to see me in real time, though, and it took a month, two months, for me to get her out in the open. So this is March, April, I'm talking about.

Livia ordered a quesadilla, I said I wasn't hungry.

"Just get something," she said. "I hate you faggy New York boys that never eat anything."

"Eating puts me to sleep."

"Alcoholic," she said, nodding and shrugging like, "Of course" or "Story of my life."

"Well fuck," I said, "I already told you all that."

"Well fuck? Did you just say *fuck* to me?"

She was eyeing me down the bridge of her nose, like she couldn't believe it, like she didn't know what she was looking at. I didn't answer, didn't know if I was supposed to or not.

"Did you just *cuss* at me?" Her eyebrows pushed a V into her forehead and I wanted to laugh again.

I said I was sorry, she turned to the waiter with this grin on her, said, "Would you like to see something, sir?" The waiter, he didn't say anything either—and it was like Livia was alone there for a second. Then she turned to me, toned down her smile and made her eyes small.

"Leon?"

"Yes?"

"What's our motto?"

I knew what she was talking about but I pretended not to. I said, "Excuse me?"

"Our motto."

Now the waiter was leaning in over his order pad, the skin pulling back from his eyes—I could see them, blue as a Nazi's. He wanted to know, Livia had his attention.

I remember the both of them waiting for me, their eyes on me, feeling a jolt shiver down through my body.

"Livia first," I said. My cock moved, saying it.

She hummed reaching across the table for me, pulled me close by the back of the neck, sucking my lip into her mouth and sliding her teeth on it, side to side.

"Such a good boy," she said.

The waiter, he started cracking up, slapping his pad against his palm and wheezing out the laughs.

"Look at that," he said.

"I'm sorry about being such a bitch," Livia told him. "I get so bad when I haven't eaten, sir."

"I bet you do," he said and then—softer, like he'd just re-membered something—"Anyway, it's like that all over."

I ordered a grilled cheese, felt calm again. All the energy in my body couldn't have run a toy truck.

When the waiter went away Livia looked around, checking out all the junk on the dark wood walls—the old-time baseball bats and hockey sticks, a newspaper cover saying, JAPS ASK PEACE, campaign banners for Kennedy, Eisenhower, Truman . . .

"Dead things turn you on?"

"I'm sorry—what?"

"There's not a picture of a living body in this whole room."

I scanned the room.

"That's the theme," I said. "There are a hundred and seven of these places across the country and if you go into any one of them you'll see exactly the same thing. The manager told me all about it before they canned his ass."

That was a lie, I'd never been there before in my life. The chain it belonged to, though, it had this mascot, Scallywag Pete—this actor done up like a filthy-looking Mark Twain. He'd get on TV saying, "Tell them Scallywag Pete sent ya!" That's why I asked Livia to meet me there, because I wanted to say it, I wanted to tell them, "Scallywag Pete sent me!" I thought it would be funny saying that. When we got there, though, I just didn't have it.

We looked around together—*Casablanca*, Lucky Lindy, base-ball gloves oiled black in their pits, *Angels with Dirty Faces*, a sinking battleship over the line "Someone Talked!"

"And none of it's real," I said. "There's not a genuine antique in here, all of it's reproduced."

"And this is the nicest place you could think to take me to?" She was rolling her glass along her lip, trailing her black lipstick on the rim, scanning me.

"You can go to Jersey," I said, "you can go to Louisiana, Nebraska, you can go to Idaho—it'll be exactly the same thing, like you never went anywhere. It's good like that."

Livia lied, too. She said she'd been in a witch cult, that she'd learned to use magic and that she'd used it to kill a boyfriend in high school. He killed himself—I found out later.

One true thing she told me was that her father beat her until she was seventeen, mostly making her stand still with her shirt off and her fingers locked behind her head while he went at her with a belt. He'd also come up out of nowhere and punch her in the back of the head, what Livia called the sneak attacks. She wasn't shy about telling me, she knew what it was worth.

After the waiter came by with our second round, Livia took a sip and whispered, "This place is fully crawling with Jews." Her shoulders were bunched up like it was all of a sudden cold in there and she was holding on to herself, rubbing the tops of her arms with her fingers.

"You're afraid of Jews?"

"There are a lot of things I'm afraid of, Leon—Jews are not one of them. I don't have anything against them, you know that, but I'm not from here—it's just, you never really get used to it."

"You get used to everything."

"I've been here three years and I'm still not. I'd really rather be just about anyplace else in the world. There's something creepy about it here—like everything's just stuck or something."

She'd moved to Poughkeepsie from Jupiter, Florida, when she was seventeen to become this guy's sub—she'd met him online too. After a few months he let two of his friends rape her and she figured out that, really, she'd been a Domme all along.

She'd been tied to a tree, it was snowing, the flakes changed in the light, they became stars, and she saw herself standing in a crater on an asteroid—she'd been sent off the earth, the earth had nothing to do with her anymore. Eventually, she landed in Queens.

"I wouldn't go anywhere else," I said. "I don't make sense anywhere else."

"You're like these people on the walls," she said. "You're all out of surprises."

I looked around—at Bogart, Amelia Earhart, Thurman Munson. "I don't think they were ever anyone's slave."

"Everyone is," she said. She smiled, told me I was pretty, said it was a shame what she was going to do to me.

"What are you going to do to me?"

Shaking her head, she put her finger to her lips, saying, "First we're going to have dinner."

My third drink came along with the food, I nursed it and Livia worked on her quesadilla, careful with the fork and knife—small pieces—not letting any of it touch the sides of her mouth. It was easy to be there, I wanted something to freeze us there. There were TV sets all over the walls, Hagler was fighting Hearns in them, in another decade, and I thought that something could have sent me back, flashed me to another year—to find everyone, to stop things happening.

The hostess went past us with two cops behind her, she sat them in the booth in front of ours, behind Livia's back—a male and a female, about my age. They didn't look like full-on mouth-breathers, exactly, but they still had the uniforms and the stupid hats. I tightened up.

"What's wrong?"

I shook my head, I shrugged.

"Speak."

"I hate those guys."

"Hmm?" with the fork sliding out from her teeth.

"The police."

She didn't like that, she asked me what I thought was protecting us from any typical ape that wanted to go off. I kept my mouth shut, Livia put her fork down, held her hand up and showed me a tiny space between her thumb and forefinger, a pinch of light with pinholes buzzing around it, slashes in the color of the world—

"We're this close," she said. "The difference between having a nice quiet dinner and everything being looted and raped and burned to the ground is this much." She pushed that little space between her fingers at me.

That space wasn't much, and what Livia said sounded right— that we lived in it.

Her name wasn't Livia. She'd named herself that on the asteroid, when she became dominant. Before that, she'd been Ellen Banks, as submissive as anyone else.

Looking between her fingers, at that space she was holding on to, I said, "Cops have nothing to do with it."

The space went away, Livia opening her hand. She picked up her fork again, cut herself a mouthful, neat, and shook her head chewing.

"Don't ever," she told me. "Don't ever try telling me you know more about it than I do. I know what I am talking about."

I believed it, that she knew what she was talking about—the sneak attacks, going into space, it gave her authority, dibs on the end of the world. Her father got his dibs in Vietnam, her whole family had me outclassed—I was selling ad space at the *Courier*.

"I'm sorry," I said. "I just don't love cops."

"And why is that?"

"Because they can do anything they want to you."

Touching the corner of her mouth with her napkin, Livia looked like she was about to laugh. "Oh, pretty," she said, "anyone can do anything they want to you."

"So what are you going to do to me?"

"Excuse me?"

"What are you going to do to me?"

Her face twisted like she'd just bitten into a cockroach and her head jerked back a little. She was eyeing me down the bridge of her nose again.

"Do you think for one second I'm going to talk about sex with you? I am not going to talk about sex with you."

"What did I do wrong?"

She wouldn't look at me and I felt like I was getting lost, like I'd stopped mattering. My eyes started to hurt and I wanted to get away from her. But I sat still, I waited.

"You don't pay attention," she said, "you don't listen." She tapped my plate with her knife. "I told you to eat. That's three times you made me tell you."

I felt the old energy starting up, beating the ache into my forearms and up through my neck. Livia didn't look like Livia anymore, her face changed, there was a shadow around it and she could've been anyone.

There was a tap, Livia was leaning her face toward me, bouncing the blade of her knife in the air over the rim of my plate. I started eating, Livia nodded, telling me, "My word has got to be law with you."

"Okay."

"Oh, sweetie," she said, "you have no idea."

"But I can learn."

"Learn faster."

The cops got up behind her, the male put some money down, and they walked past us. Livia tightened up, put the knife down and held on to the tops of her arms. She bit her lip watching them go, like she felt something behind her. Then she showed me the space between her fingers again, smiled, and made it smaller.

Out on Queens Boulevard it smelled like rain that had come and gone or was still coming and there was this haze lit orange by the streetlights. I asked Livia to tell me about the asteroid again, what it had looked like, how it felt to be so far away.

"Nobody knows you're gone," she said. "You're going to die there and the world's going to die without you. And you just hate it."

We were crossing the fourteen lanes, island to island, night traffic going east and west around us, the orange haze smearing on all the windows.

"The scariest thing is the stars so close up. They're gigantic, they're so huge, just these thick old glowing rods—all that power, it wants to just burn you all up."

We were on the last cement island, waiting for the light to change. Livia was staring out across the last three lanes, pressing the button on the lamppost, that button that doesn't do anything.

"You're so close," she said, "you can feel it hating you."

I told her I wanted to see it.

"You would," she said. "So you won't need me anymore, so you can leave me."

Chris Cinigliaro's father had the same trouble with cocaine that I did—this chemical mania, this fear of falling that was so nightmare harsh we had to drink all the way through it. I wasn't the same kind of mess as C.C.'s father, though—I stopped doing coke without killing anyone.

The great thing about coke was that we could down an ocean with it, we could drink a whole fifth or most of a liter of anything without falling asleep and then we'd walk around dreaming. Except, you understand, we'd be doing the things we dreamed instead of dreaming them.

The year I got out of high school C.C.'s father dreamed that he was stabbing his wife to death. She was no pleasure of a woman, but she was joy itself if you stood her up to her husband, who was one of these street animals in the garbage pressed-wood houses, going from job to job, delivering some shit that had nothing to do with them, cleaning places that weren't theirs—weak in the heart, always getting murdered or murdering someone else by accident.

C.C. decided to kill his father, he had the man's gun and was going around the neighborhood saying he would shoot him when he found him. That was simple show-and-tell, though, since his father was locked up waiting to make bail.

By the time his father bailed out, C.C. was waiting his turn at the Queens House of Detention for Men. He'd gone over to Reuben's place, shot him in the thigh, and Reuben had bled to death sitting on his kitchen floor. Reuben had sold C.C.'s dad the coke.

C.C. was sixteen.

Seven years later, we threw him a party.

Jenny was bartending at Hole in One, the restaurant at the Kissena golf course, so we had it there. For a week after her and Carrie had disappeared from my apartment I couldn't track down either of them. Then Jenny called saying that she'd never gotten sick, that Carrie was a liar, that Carrie's the one that needed rehab and she never wanted to talk to her again.

I never found out what really happened.

Rahmer volunteered to pick C.C. up at his aunt's place—he had a hard-on for ex-cons, twisted as a frat boy.

I tried getting someone else to drive me over but Rahmer was the only one willing to mission out to Kew Gardens—my old friend. So that was the whole ride over, this maniac, this murderer, and me.

It was prison all the way, these two talking about dishes they'd invented and trading up on fight stories—they made eggs scrambled up with mini-franks, mini-franks mixed up with macaroni and cheese, spaghetti with ketchup and mayonnaise, they said Mexicans were the most dangerous because they didn't bother trying to fight but just stabbed you, and black guys weren't as badass as they were supposed to be because they pussied up as soon as they saw their own blood.

It was all shit to me, I wasn't with them anymore.

I remember Rahmer talking about time, saying, "I was staring out at the fence during rec. It was only those fifty yards—so close you could see the girls' earrings in the cars going by, these college-looking girls. I was seeing that the fence, the fence had nothing to do with it. It wasn't holding me. You know—how easy is it to hop that fence? I was locked down by time, two years was holding me. You *serve* time. Like you're time's bitch."

I could see it getting into his face—time, the past—he had the same look on him he had those last few weeks before they sent him up, the same one he'd had when he was strolling up to those two retards calling him out by the bleachers back in high school—it was solid with an energy behind it, making his eyelids shiver.

C.C. said, "That's the shit I'm talking about, bro," and they were both nodding their heads. Then it was all silence and these two were wagging their faces at each other—sitting in a parking lot. And in that jeep there was no door for me to get out of without C.C. getting out first, so I had to sit there until they both got what they wanted out of each other.

Inside Hole in One, all the guys wanted to be from a gangster movie. They'd get C.C. around the neck with one arm and kiss him on both cheeks, telling him things like, "I know, man, I know," in these low voices like it was all a secret, nodding their heads, patting his shoulder, throwing out an arm to pull in some other guy, huddling up in threes and fours, messing each other's hair.

I said to Jenny, "Why don't they just fuck?"

"Leon?" she said.

"Yeah?"

"Why don't you just let them have fun?"

"Because what is this?"

We didn't get into it. I asked if she was still mad at Carrie and she twisted her mouth at me, shrugging.

"I don't care enough to be mad. She's back at the farm, though—I told you she would be."

I didn't know if it was true or not, there was no one to ask.

They got C.C. to the bar, all of them still managing to grab on to all the rest of them, and called for shots. It was Ron Cohen taking charge of the bar, this kid the same height as me but beefed out on steroids. His body was the kind I hated most, it seemed to vibrate, like it wanted to come apart—there was too much of it, it was supposed to be thin. He wore these bright orange-and-red-striped lifting pants that bloomed out to hide his little spindles and if you stared at them it was liable to make Ron's chemicals heat up until he lost his shit on you. I got away from him, around the corner of the bar, but he started calling to me.

"Crotch, you little prick. You're not drinking with me?"

"Why would I drink with you?" I said. "It's beneath me."

They were set up like the Last Supper, ten or twelve of them riding the front of the bar, packed thickest at the middle, with a couple of strangers off to the ends. On each side of C.C. the guys were leaning toward him like he had something to say—they had pink faces, sweaty collars, jumpy little eyes, their girls were in the background, drinking at the tables, the light softer back there—Ron's sister Deana was in it.

I'd bounced her off a wall once. She'd worked with Dara and me at Uno's and I'd shoved her at a wall in the basement face-first as hard as I could—she'd said something about Dara.

"Beneath you?" Ron said.

"Oh, absolutely."

Coming over, laughing, Ron got an arm around my shoulders and gave my body a shake, asked where I'd been and what I'd been doing. I said I'd been breaking big rocks into little rocks.

"This kid gets seven shots," he said. "Jenny—hear that? Seven shots for this kid. Seven's the holy number, Koch. Let he who has understanding understand me. Do you understand me?"

"Nope."

"Koch, you're fucked." He swung me out by my shoulders, like I was a door he was opening, raised a glass saying *salute* to everyone.

Hooting and slapping the wood, downing yellow shots, they looked like they were getting ready to do something I didn't want any part of—kick the shit out of someone or start telling each other they loved each other. Either way, it wasn't for me.

Rahmer was out on the edge of the bar crowd, scanning their faces. Some dude stumbled backward from the crowd, laughing, and Rahmer slipped out of his way. He slid back into his spot, keeping his eyes on the guy, then he scanned me and I looked away.

Jenny had seven of these yellow things lined up on the bar. I stood there waiting to be ready, to drink them, letting my chest go warm and feeling my rib cage pressing in, looking at Deana—she was a mess. Her thighs had ballooned and she'd stuffed them into these white plastic pants, the girl had on a baby-T with "Porn Star" ironed over her breasts and her belly was dimpled, hanging over the plastic waist. Her boots had four inches of platform going.

I'd tossed her into a wall one night when I should have been dreaming and she'd never told anyone. I tried to go over to her now but there were hands all over me.

Ron was saying, "Don't insult me, kid," and I told him I wasn't the entertainment. There were more hands on me than just Ron's—every step I took toward Deana, another one of them would grab my elbow or my collar, I could smell the grease on their faces, someone touched my cheek and it started itching, there was a tearing noise and the lining came out of my jacket—

There was George Tatsis holding it up, this strip of lining, waving it in my face.

"Dude, is this yours?"

I snatched Tatsis's wrist and got my fist up. Girls started screaming.

Then we were all on the move, the whole pack of us, away from the counter, away from Jenny, toward Deana—I didn't need to walk, the crowd moved me where I was supposed to go. Over the bar went Jenny, and out the door, us too, and all the girls.

Out in the driveway, I started turning, quick, one way and another, with my fists up, trying to find Tatsis—I thought he was going to come from behind and sucker-punch me.

He got his arms around me. Fuck, he was huge—I couldn't do anything about it. "Koch," he whispered, "relax, kid. Who you jumping?"

It was Ron holding me—he had on this fluffy ski jacket and I could feel how hard his chest was against my back. He said, "Who are you trying to jump? Let these boys handle it between themselves."

This island of wet grass was in the middle of the drive and we'd made a circle around it. In the middle of the circle this guy I'd never seen before was squaring off with C.C. He kept saying, "That's my girl, man!"

C.C. shrugged, reached out and smacked one of the guy's fists with the back of his hand, laughing at him. "Yeah," he said. "She's a nice girl."

They stepped toward each other and there was a crack, Ron's arms fell off me, C.C. and the other guy turned to us and I twisted. Down on the asphalt, Ron was holding on to his head.

Rahmer was standing over him with arms spread out, saying, "Who are you grabbing, motherfucker? I'll fucking kill you!"

This little flurry went by me, spun me sideways knocking my elbow—that flurry, that was Deana. She was shrieking that that was her brother and trying to get her hands in Rahmer's face. He was much too tall, all he had to do was put his palm in her face, she could never get anywhere near him. And the more she tried the more damage her platforms were doing to her brother. Ron, he got up to his knees pulling on Deana by the back of her little shirt.

Me, I just didn't want to touch any of them.

Kissena Boulevard was over there and taking it two or three blocks I'd be on Horace Harding, where there was a pay phone

to call a cab and get me out of this. I started walking. There
went that cracking sound again, there was C.C. with his back to
me swinging on someone whose legs were about to give out.
Were those Rahmer's legs? Yep. And that was Rahmer's face.
But that wasn't C.C. beating him down after all—who was that?
I didn't know. That wasn't George Tatsis, though—Tatsis was
strolling up on me.

"Are you kidding me?" getting my fists up. I looked at my
fists, dropped them, raised them again, looked around for something to hit him with.

"Dude," he said, "maybe you can sew it up or something.
Here, take this shit."

It was that lining from my jacket, the white stuffing falling
away from the black nylon.

"Are you kidding me?"

"I think you got caught on my watch, I think I grabbed
you—did you get caught on my watch?"

Something was wrong with his face—it was lopsided, it was
uneven. When I took the piece of lining from him, Tatsis
started flicking his thumb back and forth above his eye. Half the
eyebrow was missing from there.

"What did you do?"

"You can see it?"

"Yeah," I said.

"I'm touching it?"

"Yeah."

"Ah," he said. "That's bad."

Whatever was wrong with him, I was afraid he'd tell me, and
that I'd have to come up with something to say about it—
Rahmer took care of that, he went by us in his jeep, crossed
Kissena Boulevard, spun around and headed back, coming at us
full blast.

We were standing there in his beams and I thought of Deana
behind me somewhere. If Rahmer killed her she'd never get

married and tell her husband about this guy who slammed her into a wall for nothing. If Rahmer killed her I'd never be able to pay her back. But I was never going to pay her back anyway—I knew that.

There was a light I couldn't see through, metal screaming, and then the pulsing orange haze of my eyes readjusting to the darkness—there was a crash in there too.

A guy was floating in the haze, five feet above the rest of us. I closed my eyes, shook my head, saw him again. He was standing on the passenger door of Rahmer's jeep, trying to stamp out the window. The jeep had hit the curb turning, it had flipped over and slid into the parking lot on its side—everyone just stepped out of its way.

So Deana was still alive, she was alive and she was kicking one of Rahmer's headlights with her stupid platforms. Ron was trying to yank her away from it.

He was screaming, "Your baby! Your baby!"

I whispered, "Slut," tucking the jacket lining into my pocket.

C.C. snatched the guy off the side of the jeep and helped Rahmer climb out. A few of them lifted the jeep back onto its tires. When the police showed up they went right to Jenny and she said Rahmer had tried to run her over. So they arrested him.

Before they got Rahmer into the cruiser, Jenny said, "Thanks for ruining my party, asshole," and Rahmer spit in her face.

Now he was knocking his forehead against the window, saying something to me, but I couldn't hear it through the glass—the cruiser was soundproof, so animals could scream all they wanted. I went up closer, Rahmer mouthing something at me, again and again, until I could read his lips—

"Help me."

"How? What am I going to do?"

A cop said, "Get away from the car. He's got nothing to say to you."

"I'm looking right at him talking."

"I think you better stand away from the car."

I was sober, I was white, I wasn't carrying anything—so I said, "Hey, Detective, maybe I don't give a shit what you think."

"And I know I don't give a shit what you think," he said. "Now stand away from my car or I'll lock your ass up."

They were forever saying things like that, like, "You want to get locked up tonight?" Like it was a choice—if you were stupid about choosing they had places to take you. They could take you if they wanted.

I was afraid of them and afraid for Rahmer—I didn't want to be an animal, I didn't want Rahmer to be an animal. But there he was, hands behind his back, still mouthing at me—even while C.C. was pulling me away, even after he'd put me inside Rahmer's jeep. He kept saying I had to help him, all the way across the drive, through his window.

Even with my jacket hooded over my head, Rahmer wouldn't stop saying it. What was I going to do for him—lift the jeep up? Throw it? Lift up cops? Could I lift cops for him?

I couldn't even get Ron's arms off me when I wanted to, I couldn't even stop myself shaking.

"They're letting us take the jeep," C.C. told me. I could feel the cold coming off him—he had on this M.C. and the leather stayed cold. I grabbed on to myself.

The windshield was spiderwebbed and I asked what made him think the glass wouldn't come flying in our faces.

"It could happen," he said. "What do you want me to do about it?"

I knew he'd never take me home—it couldn't happen that way, it couldn't stop. He got on the LIE going the wrong way, going east, fast, toward Bell Boulevard.

The bars were dead that night, there were just the old men out there and some of the little kids, these punk-asses that hung around by the 7-Eleven, where the ambulance always parked, talking about all the people they were going to "cap" if they fucked with them. One of them asked us to buy them beer, C.C. told him to go home.

He brought a six-pack of Heineken back to Rahmer's jeep and sat there drinking them in the parking lot. I wanted to drink, but I didn't want to start talking—I waited.

C.C. was talking about Rahmer, asking me if his parole was up yet. I tried to do the math, counting months, years, but they swirled away from me, I said, "I don't know."

"It's shit, bro. If his P.O. violates him, my dad could get out before he does." Getting a boot up against the dash, C.C. leaned his seat back, telling me, "They turned him down the first time he came up but they won't turn him down twice. He'll say he's clean now and how he's accepted the Lord as his personal savior—you can kill anyone you want to if you don't plan it out."

"Do you still want to kill him?"

First he blew through his teeth, then he pushed his hair back behind his ear. "Kill your father?" he said. "It's too big. Do you know what that is?"

"Nope."

"I'm not saying I shouldn't. If I did then maybe it would stop happening. It keeps happening—you know what I'm talking about?"

I did know, and that's why I didn't answer him. I knew he meant that his father killing his mother was still happening—

"He's stabbing her in the neck, bro—he stabs her in her fucking neck! He stabs her in her fucking neck!"

It was happening in his eyes and he was showing it to me. I reached out for him, I dug my thumbs into his eyes, because he shouldn't have shown me—until he screamed, twisting his face away, until he caught my hand in his mouth.

There was that cracking sound, because tiny bones were breaking, and my arm went palsy, shivering, hairs jumping up, me watching it—the side of my hand in his mouth with his teeth getting into the skin, his face wagging, head side to side like a dog's head.

After that I remember waking up in the parking lot with C.C. on my chest punching me in the face. All the beatings I'd had anything to do with happened so fast there wasn't anything to see. Or it had been a bunch of guys and I couldn't see it happening because I kept my face covered. This time, though, with my arms under C.C.'s knees, I got to watch the whole thing.

It was like an experiment—if C.C. wanted my face to go to one side, he'd punch it on the other side. I tried to keep my eyes open but they closed themselves every time he hit me. And when I opened them up again there was nothing but bursts of light.

I think he mainly wanted to break my nose, because he kept slamming his fist into it, but it was like rubber—it must have been cool for him doing that, keep hitting this thing that keeps springing back for him to hit it again.

When he asked me if I'd had enough, his fist was up behind his ear, bouncing at the end of his arm, getting ready, and I didn't know what to tell him—I knew how I'd feel when it was over because I knew how I'd felt before it started.

He didn't ask me again, just got up off me and disappeared. I could hear the jeep going away and I stayed there on the asphalt with my arms where he'd left them.

I remember lying there thinking about everyone, that they should find me there, that Jenny should come by and spit in my face, and Deana could grind her platforms in it, stomp on it—again and again, all night. Then those kids from the 7-Eleven could come and empty a garbage can on me. And Rahmer, Rahmer could run me over with his jeep. C.C.'s mom could come, too, and do whatever she wanted, she could drop all of Bayside on me, right on my face, shove it in my mouth, the whole thing, plus the county of Queens—all of it, everyone.

8

Livia's dog Moses got killed when she was fifteen, it was the sorest gripe she ever had with the universe. I think she could have taken the rest of her life pretty well if that dog hadn't been smeared all over some interstate, if he could've gone quietly. That's when she was still Ellen Banks.

Right up front, Livia warned me, "If you ever say a word against my dog." She meant that would be it for us, the whole thing.

I promised to respect her dead pet, I knelt in front of the futon, kissed the tops of Livia's feet, flowing on codeine.

"Will you stay?" looking up at her.

"Look at me."

"I am."

"If I stay, you're not seeing a single one of those people again. Do you understand?"

"Yes, Mistress."

She crossed her arms under her chest, straightening her neck, and pouted down at me.

"Oh, sweetie. Look what they did to you."

There was a purple crescent on each side of my nose, where my nostrils had gone flat against my face, both eyes were black, two fingers in a cast, and my teeth throbbing through the codeine haze.

"I had it coming," I said.

She reached down, touched my cheek, telling me, "I'm the only one who hurts my boy."

She moved her stuff in the next day. I called Ortiz about it, he was the only one—no one else had earned knowing. Rahmer, the girls, there was no trusting any of them. I worked, paid rent, paid taxes—it's all I owed anything.

Every morning, Livia would say, "Do you think you could ever be as good a dog as my Moses?" and I'd tell her, "I try." She'd shake her head and make a sniffing noise.

She'd buried Moses in her father's yard and the old fucker had laid off her for a while—even he couldn't deny what kind of a good dog Moses had always been.

If we ever got married, we'd have to go dig up that dog and bring him back here.

Livia would say to herself, "I'm not leaving you there forever," and, "Any day now, Moses."

She'd crawl up my stomach in bed, hold my cheeks between her fingers, spit in my mouth and ask, "Do you like that, pretty?" I'd give her one answer or another and Livia would giggle, telling me, "Oh, pretty, yes and no are fully the same thing."

Think of a prop, Livia had it—the whips and the crops, every last boot, high heel, gag, noose, pin-sharp fangs she'd wear over her own teeth . . . The time travel, though, that was all me.

The idea was she'd sneak up behind me and punch me in the back of the head, she'd be her father and I'd be her—I mean, you understand, who she'd been as a teenager—Ellen Banks, down on one knee holding my head, the beige walls covered with the old fucker's bullshit diplomas and framed Polaroids of him with the PTA chair and the heads of the chamber of commerce going back fifteen years.

He'd be standing over me calling me cunt with my Moses turning to bone out in the yard.

That slam in the back of the head, I begged her for it, but Livia was against it from day one.

"A punch is too blunt," she said. "Blunt isn't sexy, it isn't erotic." She had on her rubber gloves, her hair tied back in a blue bandana. "You know my father used the belt on me, too—why don't we do that?"

"You weren't as scared of it."

"It was a different kind of scared," she said. "And anyway, punching a boy in the face doesn't sound hot to me at all," wiping a bead of sweat off her nose with her shoulder. "Precision is hot—a slap in the face, a snap of the whip." She rinsed the suds off a salad bowl, put it in the rack, and took a wine glass from the soapy water, telling it, "He wants me to sock him in the face. Where on earth does he come from?"

"Not in the face," I said. "Who said anything about my face?"

"Why don't I just kick you in the balls?"

"No thanks on that one, princess."

"You see?" she told the glass. "He thinks he knows all about this." Livia smiled at me. "I've got news for you, skippy."

"It's just a mind game."

"Don't I know that?"

"Well fuck, Livia."

"Do not *cuss* at me!"

"Sorry."

She snatched a dish towel off the refrigerator door, tossed it to me saying, "Make yourself useful."

"My God," my grandmother told my mother, "we never even thought about that. We just did what we did."

She meant oral sex, that no one had ever given it to her in her life, though she was a hot little thing in her time—I've seen pictures.

My grandmother had been dead six years when my mother told us the story. My stepbrother Alex was in town from San Francisco so the family met up at this Mexican place on Union Turnpike and we got housed on margaritas.

"I mean," my mother was saying, "it wasn't even in their frame of reference. Can you imagine?"

She wanted an answer, she was looking around at us with her eyes wide and her hands out. But there wasn't an answer, we couldn't imagine, and Livia tugged on my shirt under the table. I leaned closer to her, nonchalant, and she whispered, "I cannot hear another word about your grandma's ya-ya."

I wanted Ortiz to be there, to send the conversation some-where else—he was good like that, he always knew what to say. I hadn't heard from him in two months. Livia didn't mind me calling him, I'd told her so many good things about the kid, but the fucker just stopped calling me back.

Sucking back a sip, I said, "Now Ortiz, there's a man that eats some pussy." They all looked over. "Iron and steel," I told them, "eyes-deep in some of the sweetest gash west of the Rockies. Rocky Mountain pussy, now that's some pussy, but Idaho poo-na, that's the real magic—they've got some snapping gyro out there."

Livia whispered, "Leon," and that meant to stop talking.

A few hours before that, she'd pissed down the back of my neck in the shower.

My great-great-grandfather stabbed a Cossack to death with a butcher's knife on a street outside of Minsk in 1894—that's when they called it White Russia. He got killed for it, shot through the neck, and had a son a few months later who came here in 1907 and married a woman who killed herself in 1936. They'd taken out her appendix and sanitized the wound with hydrochloric acid. The second night after the operation the burning got her out of bed—she wasn't even old yet, she was thirty-one—tearing at the bandages. She had thick black hair and a ballerina's neck, jumping out a hospital window in the middle of the night.

I knew her husband until he was ninety-five and I was sixteen. He said Al Capone used to collect from his clothing store before he moved to Chicago, when he was still a lieutenant on the Lower East Side. Capone used to tell his guys, "Leave Victor alone, Victor's a good Jew," is what Victor told me.

"Honestly," my mother was saying, "I don't see what's wrong with a simple, well-kept triangle." She meant how a woman groomed her pubic hair—that's where the conversation had gone to.

"Let's get Uncle Harvey's opinion on that," Alex said, meaning my stepfather. A pale, raised line ran from ear to ear across the top of Alex's head, where they'd cut it open to get at the tumors inside.

"I think we should get *Livia's* opinion," Harvey said—he was trying to bring her into the clan.

"Please," she said, "I'd rather not, sir."

"She'd rather not, *sir!*" Harvey laughed. Livia grabbed my wrist under the table.

A few rounds later, Alex was chanting, "Even Uncle Harvey wants to party, even Uncle Harvey wants to party," while Harvey danced in the aisle with a girl from another booth and my mother let loose with that stiff-faced crying she had, straightening up in her seat and sniffing like she was breathing up her pride, not lifting a hand to wipe the tears away.

Livia gave me a yank, whispered that she needed air, so we went outside and smoked. Through the glass storefront we watched Alex dancing with Harvey, the girl from the other booth between them, my brother Greg's girlfriend saying something to my mother, my mother nodding, patting her hand.

"Alex used to be a rapper," I told Livia. She had her arms crossed under her chest, holding on to the tops of her arms. "He called himself Spatula Freebase. That was years ago, when he could still hear in both ears, but he's still pretty good."

"I'm glad for him," she said staring out at the parking lot. "I really am."

"There's a little piece of gold in his right eyelid so he can close it when he wants to."

"My mother had cancer the last time I saw her," Livia said, still staring into the dark. "She was okay, though. She did just fine."

She hadn't seen the woman in ten years.

Livia turned to me, scanned my face, and slid up against me, hugging me around my neck.

"I'd just love to put them all on a boat or some damn thing," she said. I could feel her whispering through all the tiny bones in my ear. "We could just put them all away on a boat and forget about them, we won't ever remember a thing."

When my grandmother died it was like she was trying to scream all the energy out of her body once and for all. She was in a corridor, in a wheelchair. All the old women were out there, the nurses were cleaning their rooms, these giant island women, these foreigners—we hated them.

The old women kept howling no matter what their families

did. The daughters and sons, the nieces, grandkids, they were bending down to them, crouching, they knelt at their feet, but nothing stopped the screaming. They were madwomen, two rows of them, left and right, trying to make the scariest death masks they could, their mouths wide open and their faces shivering in the white fluorescence.

My grandmother kept her mouth shut at first, just wore her face hard and let the tears make their way down the creases in her cheeks, like it was beneath her to even look like a screamer. Then, like someone told her it was time, she let loose her howl, let go of her elbows, grabbed the arms of the wheelchair, and screamed until the electricity shut off.

She froze like that, with her mouth open, so it always seemed to me that she died right in the middle of the scream. And I thought that when she died she was so crazy that her soul had gone crazy too. It was Livia who taught me otherwise.

"The scream ended when your grandma died," she'd said. "So the middle was halfway back from there. And the beginning was when it was."

I was dozing with my head on her thigh.

"Her soul isn't crazy. No matter what they do, nothing ever happens to your soul."

I was playing with her clit ring, gently sliding the bead side to side. Livia had almost no bush at all, just a little landing strip— she thought anything more was disgusting.

It took a while before she stopped crying, before we could go back inside the restaurant. Alex and my mother were arguing. She'd been talking about how her mother had died and she called the nurses black savages.

"They were human beings," Alex was saying.

"Tell that to my mother. They terrorized her right to the last minute."

"How?" Alex said. "By being black?"

It went back and forth a few times, then it was Alex's turn to go get some air and it was quiet for a minute after that. Livia filled her glass from the pitcher of margaritas, brought it up, and sipped at it until there was nothing left. Then she did it again.

"I apologize if we're making you uncomfortable," Harvey told her.

"Oh," she said. "I'm fine, sir. I'm just fine."

"When you don't get together very often it can be—" He did a thing with his hand, a little drum roll in the air. "It can be emotional."

"I think it's just fine that you all can get everything off your chests like this. My father would just beat the living shit out of me." No one said a thing. Livia looked around and giggled, she shrugged her shoulders. "At least he never tried to fuck me."

"Well," Greg said, "here's to that."

Livia scanned him, she smirked. My brother raised his glass to her.

"Fuck yes, I'll drink to that," she said and we all brought our glasses up, we all toasted to Livia never being raped by her father.

Outside, Alex was dancing with himself. I watched him through the glass storefront, his head cocked to his shoulder, one hand over his ear and the other one pointing at the sky, his body swaying side to side.

"Get a load of Freebase," I said and everyone took a look, all of us with our own sort of laugh.

"He's so odd," Livia said.

"He tried to rob a liquor store once," I told her. "He got lost on the way."

"He would."

He was bending over sideways, both hands over his ears, an elbow to the sky, starting to shake.

"He used to come home and find his mom with her head in the oven," I whispered. "She's okay now, though."

"Of course she is."

We kept smiling at Alex flinching around out there until he went into a spin and disappeared from the window, until the seizure took him off his feet and spread him twitching along the pavement. When we got to him, his eyes were rolled back white, the lids shivering over them.

A crowd started coming out of the restaurant, Harvey yelling for them to get back, to call an ambulance, my brother holding Alex's head still. Livia grabbed my wrist with one hand and covered her mouth with the other.

I watched his eyes—a glimpse of iris flashed out from under the thin bump of gold in his eyelid and rolled away again. His mouth started twisting with a stubborn, angry groan coming out. I thought he was trying to scream.

I was coming out of the bathroom brushing my teeth when Livia punched me in the back of the head. I'd heard her say, "Ummm" behind me, looked over my shoulder and saw this little flurry of light, then a flash of black, then red and yellow spots bursting all over the room. I grabbed the back of my head, spitting toothpaste.

It had been a few weeks since she'd shot down my time-travel idea, but clearly she had reconsidered—Livia was generous like that.

"Cunt," she said. "Put your hands down."

I put them down, let them hang at my sides, held on to my toothbrush.

Something squeaked behind me—Livia's flip-flops—then there was another black flash and a rumbling in my ears like water rushing. I dropped to one knee, dropped the toothbrush, held on to my elbows.

"I said put your hands down, cunt. Why are you making me do this?"

I shook my head no.

"Don't shake your head at me, cunt. I want an answer."

Her voice was flat, dead. I didn't know where she was in her mind or how far she'd go and I was scared of her for the first time—it's what I'd wanted all along.

"Are you going to answer me, cunt?"

Tick-tock.

There was a hand on the back of my neck, pushing me down until the side of my face was pressed against the wood and I could only see the room with one eye. Closing my eyes, there were beige walls under diplomas, Moses yelping under the screech of brakes, Moses quiet in the ground, out past a row of palms.

"When are you going to learn how to conduct yourself like a human being, you fucking whore?"

I wanted to tell him that there was no such thing as a whore, but I didn't know how to put it yet—there was no answer, there was no place to go, just the floor in my face, the flashes of black . . .

And trees, woods turning black, his thumb pushing in behind my ear . . .

"This time you're going to remember it, Ellie."

"Only for the rest of my life, faggot."

"What did you say, cunt?"

"I said fuck you."

By the end of the spring one of us had given the other one crabs. We tore our throats up swearing against each other but we'll never know which way it really went, who gave what to who.

Whoever was guilty, Livia went back to Florida to live with her mother, a few miles from where her father had raised her. They'd made peace, Livia and her mom, peace enough to wait together—for the old fucker to drop dead.

I named a drink in her honor—gin and lemonade. Other people have mixed that, sure, but I named it, it's called a Livia.

What was so perfect about a Livia was that you couldn't taste the gin. I didn't have anything against the taste of gin but, still, it was hard to drink enough to get me anywhere before I threw up. The lemonade stung your tongue and your body didn't know what you were doing to it until you'd already done it.

Ortiz finally called and I told him about my invention, that it was my way of saying sorry to her, whether it was my fault or not—he said he wanted to come visit. He'd just lost some kind of computer-graphics job and he had plenty of time on his hands to "see the old neighborhood, look around . . ."

I thought I'd solved my problems with a special shampoo and this tiny yellow comb but the crabs were back in a week so I shaved myself clean and boiled all my underwear. It took four pots, one on each burner, the whole kitchen choked up with steam and me stabbing the boxers back under the water with a wooden spoon when they'd bubble up with hot air.

Ortiz was still passed out on the futon when I got the water boiling, the racket woke him up.

"Are you kidding me?" he called. "I haven't eaten breakfast since the kangaroos ran the government."

"There's no food in here, son, but come feast your eyes."

Coming up behind me through the steam, Ortiz said, "It's a fucking bathhouse in here," and then he got a load of what was cooking and jumped back to the kitchen door. He pressed his forehead to the door frame laughing and said, "Can you go to hell any faster?"

I'd had to borrow two pots from Aranov, down the hall, one of them this giant cast-iron sucker you could've boiled a man's head in. He asked me what I needed the pots for and he didn't mind when I told him, just laughed and made me have a beer with him. Sundays were a drunk day for a lot of the men in my building, they'd be arguing out in the courtyard, drinking vodka from thermoses while their wives chased after their kids.

"You're not partying out back?" I said.

"With the Russians?" He made a face like he was about to spit. "For two drinks they kick their children, they slap their wife in her face."

"You're Russian."

He held up his hand to stop me, said, "Not like that." Then he raised his beer to me saying, "Vodka is shit."

It was true, I nodded.

"Today will be peaceful," he told me. "My wife will take the girls to the beach."

"Cool."

He shrugged. "My wife is whore like yours."

"I'm not married."

"Still, Valeria is a whore."

"Sorry."

"For who?" Aranov grabbed his crotch and started laughing again.

The next day Ortiz and me went back to Bayside to see the

house he grew up in, Ortiz driving us over in his rental—I'd never driven in my life. It was maybe eleven in the morning, we had these forty-four-ounce nightmare cups from White Castle, full of Livias.

The house was one lawn, two front doors, two more on the sides, four driveways, two garages, three stories, four families—brickface on the bottom half, white aluminum slats across the top—a mimosa tree dying out front, limbs sagging away from the sun, the mouths of the blossoms withered shut.

My mother and Harvey still lived halfway down that block, so this whole production didn't thrill me, but I was trying hard to accommodate Ortiz. We parked across the street drinking and he stared at the house for a few minutes.

"I just wanted to look at it," he said. "You know, you see people doing a thing like this and they're always saying, 'I don't know what I expected to get out of this.' But I know what I'm getting out of it—I can feel it."

He was blowing his smoke out the window. I wanted to smoke, too, but I wasn't feeling up to it. I'd developed this coldness in my bones that wouldn't go away. There was this shivering in my lungs all the time, my thighs ached, and I couldn't feel myself when I pissed.

"Great!" he said, squinting out at the house, nodding. "That'll about do it."

"Great," I said. "I'm freezing. And I'm sure my fucking stepdad'll come prancing by any second."

We started gliding down the avenue toward P.S. 203, past Queensborough. Ortiz slowed down and opened the door, leaned his head out.

This kid was magnificent, he was puking out of the door and driving at the same time—it was all the old magic.

Me, I didn't care what happened next. The guy had one hand on the wheel and one hand on the open window and he was letting go into the street, his face practically touching the damned asphalt. It was making me scream—

"Ortiz, you maniac! You are the fucking greatest thing I've ever seen! You're a fucking giant!"

I was way down in my seat, kicking the dashboard and hacking. Then Ortiz wasn't there anymore and I felt his side of the car roll over something, me thinking, Ortiz jumped out, we hit a cat, I'm going to crash into that fence.

Of course there wasn't any cat—that cat, that was Ortiz's head, and those were children out there. I knew that.

A cat was just a shape things took, these bursts of darkness scurrying under things, in the corners of my eyes—like when I came home and saw a cigarette burning on the floor in the dark by the TV and pressed my boot down on the orange glow. I crushed Livia's finger and it was a cat's tail, it was a cat screaming.

The car rolled up the little hill to the school yard and wedged itself under the bottom of the chain-link fence. I turned off the ignition, pulled up the brake. I didn't need to pull up that brake, the car wasn't going anywhere, but it seemed like I had to just because Ortiz wasn't there to do it.

I walked over by where he was and sat on the curb.

Most of the suicides I've known were accidental—O.D.s and car crashes and whatever. They all seemed to know it was coming and wouldn't take so much as a breath to make it stop, just dragged it out like torture. Ortiz, though, he had balls enough to say that's enough already and stop fucking around once and for all.

He ran his own head over with his car. To this day they'll say it was an accident, that Ortiz was retarded in a way, but I knew him all my life—he saw the tire and he went for it.

Even sitting down on that curb, staring into the mess, I respected what it took to do it up like that, that thing Ortiz had in him that I'd never seen in anyone else—Ortiz had class.

Me, I sat there, I waited. I didn't have to throw up, I didn't have to finish my Livia, I didn't have to do anything. People were going to come and take control of the situation—medical professionals, officers of the law. They were going to clean up, get to the bottom of things once and for all. Ortiz wouldn't need these people. They were coming for me.

9

The streets were blocked off down to the river and there were cops on every corner. Past the barricades crowds packed the streets three blocks deep—you couldn't see the water past all those bodies but you could see the city out over their heads, a little gray battleship in the steady haze.

I wanted to stay in Rahmer's jeep, in the air-conditioning, with Cali on my lap and her bare feet on top of mine. Her feet were ice-cold, they were smooth, tiny—she'd rub them fast on top of mine and let loose this little squeal whenever she caught a chill. Cali was always freezing, her body had nothing to keep the heat in.

We headed down Vernon Boulevard past the Con Ed plant, past Queensbridge Park, turned left onto Forty-fifth Avenue and kept going until Rahmer found a space. Mobs were heading west on both sides of the street, moms and dads and little kids—Puerto Ricans, Indians, blacks, Pinays and Pinoys, Khmers, Pakis, Koreans . . . They carried lawn chairs under their arms, radios and coolers, mini-barbecues . . .

I wanted Rahmer to pull out and take us back to the beach, head us east, away from the cops and the barricades, those crowds, the river and the city.

I said, "Look at them."

"That's the point, tiger—can you smell it?"

"I'm choking on it."

"Aww," Cali said, making a baby voice. "No one's gonna hurt you."

I'd have told her to shut up, but she pressed down, twisting the balls of her feet on top of mine. I felt my teeth with my tongue, I held my breath.

The lock on the passenger door was busted from when Rahmer'd flipped it over, we had to wait for him to come around and unlock it from the outside. The heat broke my heart as soon as the door opened. Cali was moving around in my lap, buckling her Tevas.

"Hurry up off me," I said. "The bones in your ass are killing me."

"Don't kid yourself, Koch."

Rahmer laughed helping her down. Grabbing my sneakers off the junk pile in the back I could still feel Cali's body all over me, still felt the cold coming off her.

We got in line with the crowd, everyone on the street moving at the same pace, like someone had decided it for us before we got there—except the little kids, they'd chase each other howling through the lines and we'd slow down to keep from tripping over them. Salsa or merengue or whatever was booming from the radios and people yelled to each other across the street from different parts of the lines.

We got bottlenecked at the barricade, the cops making us squeeze by on either side of it. There was a canal on our left behind a torn-up fence, this place where they'd blown a hunk out of the island and let the river come in two blocks between a pair of rotting docks. Out at the ends of the docks two cranes stuck out of the water on concrete platforms. One had its arm pointing north, the other one pointed south. Kids were climbing around on them maybe ten feet over the water.

"Don't those little fuckers have parents?" I said.

"Don't call them that," Cali said. "They're babies."

Rahmer stopped, grabbed the camera from his book bag and took a shot of them.

"That's where we need to be."

"That's a death trap," I said. "That's a death trap out there."

Cali gave me her baby voice again and Rahmer grabbed me around the shoulders, telling me, "You'll thank me later."

The first opening we came to in the fence had a cop in it. He didn't say anything, just shook his head no and waved us off with his baton. We could see whole crews of people out behind the fence, right past the cop's shoulder—families cooking and dancing on the bank, those kids screwing around on the docks and out on the cranes. We stood there eyeing them, trying to think of a way to put it.

"You can't be here," the cop said.

"Where?" Rahmer said. "Where I'm standing? Can I be where I'm standing?"

"You should take it easy."

"No—there's fifty people that can be in there, but not me? Where else can't I be? Can I be where I'm standing?"

I could've gotten that cop to let us into the canal—I had a press I.D. from the *Courier* and any cop in Queens knew the paper took their side on everything. I didn't want to help, though, didn't want any part of those ancient docks or those smashed-up platforms over the river—they scared me shitless.

Rahmer found another hole, though, even closer to the river, and we were in.

Rahmer couldn't shake the idea of that cop—we could feel it, Cali and me, the hate coming off him. We could see the muscle working in his jaw, his eyes going smaller and smaller, and it wasn't safe to even talk for a while.

As we headed out to one of the crane platforms, the planks on the dock teetered under us. There were spaces where two or three of them were missing at a stretch and we had to make our way balancing on the long supports. We could see the water swirling around the pilings, dark green for half a foot and then solid black. We heard the parents behind us, shouting over the dance music, calling to their kids from the riverbank.

We heard, "Aku! Aku, how'd you get out there?"

"I walked!"

"Well, you can walk yourself back here then!"

We went to the front of the platform and Rahmer started setting up his tripod. Cali and me sat down and hung our feet off the edge. A section of concrete had fallen in, you could see the white of it through the water, and brown steel bars twisted down around our legs from the broken edge.

"I didn't want to sneak in," Rahmer said. He was crouching at his camera, squinting at the city through the lens. "One time I just want them to let me in—I mean, just *let* me." Cali scratched his leg, he shook his head and looked at us. "I might really be getting too tired of this."

"Don't say that."

"Do you think I'm lying?"

"No," I said, "but don't say that."

Ortiz was dead a month and if he could do it we could all do it—he'd gone and shown us something, you had to respect that.

I didn't sob or quit drinking or put my fist through a window—I didn't do anything, I waited. It made too much sense. Afterward things came back to me that I thought I should've noticed, but it got obvious pretty quick that going back and noticing things wasn't going to make any difference.

That last morning I introduced Ortiz to Aranov on the elevator in my building and Aranov introduced him to his wife.

"This is Valeria," he said. "My wife."

"A pleasure," Ortiz said.

She nodded and smiled and Aranov said, "She sleeps with black man." Valeria closed her eyes. "Who knows," Aranov said, "maybe she likes this."

"Don't let it get you," Ortiz told him. "It's all cunts and cocks, my friend. And two ways about it there are not."

Then he killed himself and I still had a job to go to and an apartment to go to after that.

He kept showing up when I dreamed, sometimes his skull was pushed in over his left eye, sometimes I couldn't see him at all, just felt him around me.

I'd tell him, "You really stuck the fucking landing, huh, kid?" but he'd never say a thing—he didn't know me anymore.

I started covering all the car crashes, it was always some child at the wheel. One Tuesday in June an ambulance blowing a light on Francis Lewis Boulevard hit a Jetta and killed a pair of twin sisters. There wasn't any emergency, the EMT just got off on blowing lights, hearing his sirens. He was twenty-two.

"They were my angels," their mother told me when I called. "They were my life."

It's like she was talking to me from inside a movie, I just took it all down.

"I don't know how my God has done this to me."

The twins hadn't died together, the driver had survived. I checked her status twice a day with the City Hospital at Elmhurst and they upgraded her that Friday from critical to stable. She died over the weekend.

I lost track of her mother for a few seconds. When I could listen again she was saying, "And this thing is happening and I don't even know? My babies are dying and I don't even know?"

That's when the machines in my apartment started hissing in the floors and the walls and I tried to stay out as much as possible. Then none of my bars would let me in anymore so I unplugged the refrigerator and everything else that made noise, wrapped the smaller stuff in towels, and every night I'd buy a bag of ice at the 7-Eleven. That worked until I passed out with the oven on at full broil—I'd been trying to make toast.

It's Rahmer and Cali who woke me up, we had plans to go to the beach—they'd been dragging me around with them all over the place since Ortiz checked out, I pretended I wasn't home most nights. When I did answer the door, I never thanked them, I told them to fuck off, and they took me with them anyway—they weren't asking.

There wasn't any lecture when Rahmer realized what had happened with the oven, he just went around opening windows and put the fan in the kitchen—you could see heat waves coming out of there, the air gone slick and blurry. Then Cali said she'd wait for us out in the jeep, she said my place stunk.

"What did you expect?" I said. "People stink."

Cali was staring at me in my underwear and it felt like I'd just smacked her in the mouth, like she was from some higher race.

I started laughing, telling her, "Look, how nice the place is airing out."

"Take a shower, Leon."

Sunset made the sky quiver, it was pink streaked with orange and the bottoms of the clouds glowed red like they were floating on fire. All the windows across the river had the sky burning in them too—the buildings seemed to sway in it.

This couple had set themselves up next to us with a cooler of beers. They had the cooler between them and the girl had a baby in her lap. I heard each new beer crack open and hiss like a song that kept starting and stopping. They must have been there half an hour when the guy asked me for a cigarette.

I said, "Sorry, man, I'm running low." I'd been chaining like a fiend waiting for this thing to be over with.

"Trade you a beer," he said.

"Okay."

"You trade him from your half," the girl said.

I was staring out at the row of barges docked across the river, Cali giving that perfect face to the corner of my eye—I wouldn't look at her. The guy cracked the can open for me, was handing it to me.

"Wait," he said and poured some of the beer into the river. I thought he was doing the dead-homey thing, but he took a pint bottle of Dewar's from the cooler and poured some into the can, smiling at me.

"That's your boilermaker."

"Hardcore," I said.

He lifted the bottle to me, grinning, and we started in. His name was Kelly—we made friends right away—and that was Tia, his wife, and Kelly Jr.

"How much time we got?" he asked Tia.

"Do I have a watch?"

"About an hour," Rahmer said, snapping away at the ships passing by—yachts, pleasure cruisers, cutters, historical jobs with three sails.

"We can both get a buzz on if you want to split those reds with me."

"All right."

He fixed me another boilermaker and I swirled it around.

"What do you think they do with that?" He was looking back at the crane.

"Nothing," I said. "They don't do anything with it, it's rusted solid."

He took another cigarette. "I mean, what is it?"

I eyed the crane, made sure it was what I thought it was, and told Kelly. I pointed out all the old warehouses along the banks, covered in soot, shuttered up in the dusk. Kelly looked around, reached down and grabbed one of the steel bars coming out from where the platform had crumbled, rubbing his thumb on it.

"My dad could've worked here."

"Let me get another?"

Rahmer said, "Check out this one," and we saw a pirate ship floating by.

We couldn't believe it, we started laughing—it had the skull and crossbones, the cannons, the whole thing. The crew were all dressed up, they waved swords at us from the deck.

Kelly shook his head at it. "A man's got his own pirate ship," he said. "Who's he even got to pirate?"

"It's probably not one person," Cali said. "It's probably Disney or something."

"Who's Disney got to pirate?" He reached into the cooler and Tia grabbed his arm.

"You see? You see?" she said. "Now you're getting into mine."

He pulled his hand back, nudged me with his elbow. "Watch she won't drink but two beers anyway."

She looked like she could handle a few, she was big for a Pinay, but I hadn't seen her touch one yet.

"Tia," I said, "can I get one of yours?"

"Sure you can." She smiled, I reached across Kelly and grabbed a fresh one.

"Here she goes," Kelly said. "Here she goes." He jiggled the pint in front of me. "Let me top that."

It was dark when we all stood up. There was nothing on the water but the whiteness of the moon and nothing in the sky but the half-moon and a few pinprick stars. You couldn't see anything else through the glare of the city—it had an orange halo around it, it had an atmosphere. Rahmer swore he could see Mars up there but none of us could tell which pinprick he was pointing at.

The crowd went quiet on the shore, Tia was whispering to her baby, "Wake up, precious. It's time."

"How deep you think the river is?"

"It's not even a river," Cali whispered. "It's the Atlantic."

"What?"

"It's called a tidal strait. It's a part of the ocean."

A man's voice called for attention, it boomed through the quiet. It was a cop on the shore with a megaphone, calling us back.

"You are illegally trespassing. Clear the docks or you will be arrested."

No one moved, just looked back at the cops in the dark. He said it again—we were illegal, we were trespassing, we would be arrested.

People started making their way along the docks, kids climbed down off the cranes. Kelly picked up his cooler and started to follow Tia off the platform onto the dock. He stopped and looked back at us.

Rahmer said, "You want to get locked up tonight?"

"The area is condemned," the cop said. "Clear the area or you will be arrested." He had a team with him, their uniforms blending into the darkness of the mob, you could see the glint of their badges.

"It's not the same show from back there," I said.

"I've got a son," Kelly told me. He opened the lid of the cooler, handed me a beer, and shot the last of the whiskey.

"Cheers," he said, chucking the bottle over the river.

"A pleasure."

Three cops were coming toward us up the dock when the show started. They froze under the first blast, the crowd cheering from the shore. We turned our backs on the cops, watching the fire spread across the dark. We could feel the concussions against our faces, we screamed at it—the shore screamed, too, all of them, everyone clapping their hands and stomping the ground.

The flashes burned white, then faded out, then new ones blew up where the others had been, all of it glowing between stretches of blackness. I heard the cops' voices behind me, and the screams of the crowd, but I kept staring at the fire, kept my eyes open, until they hurt, until I saw stars, all around me, right in my face—pulsing orange rods.

Livia had said it hated us, that it wanted to burn us up. But I was right there, I was right there scanning it, and it had nothing in it to hate us with—it didn't know we were there. The hate was ours, we'd burn right here, all on our own. The rest was voodoo, nonsense.

Rahmer was laughing, the cops were on the platform and he was laughing at them. He tipped his camera and tripod off the broken edge, just let it go.

"I'm under arrest!" he yelled to the shore. "I'm arrested!"

He had his fists in the air, the sky cracking over our heads, raining down streams of light, orange smoke drifting across the river.

Rahmer put his hands behind his back, shouting, "This is for my safety as well as yours!" The cops didn't cuff him, though, just put a hand on each shoulder and walked him onto the dock.

Rahmer was up ahead of us between two of the cops, I had one behind me and Cali in front of me. I stopped at a hole in the dock, stood still on the long beam with the river on either side, Cali reaching her hand out from the other side of the hole.

"One foot in front of the other," she said. "Don't look down."

New music was coming from the radios as the cops walked us into the crowd on the shore, not dance music anymore—a symphony, the explosions were set to it, a cymbal crashed and the sky quivered behind a dozen burning spiderwebs.

There were hands all over us as the crowd closed in. Flaming zeros spread across the night while someone pulled on the collar of my T-shirt, yanked my arm—they were waving their hands in our faces, yelling, and I grabbed Cali's hand and got ahead of her, twisted us through the bodies.

The whole shore was noise—the shouts and cheers, the drums beating, the bomb blasts in the air—I couldn't tell one from another. By the time I realized what the crowd was doing they'd already done it, they'd gotten Rahmer away from the cops. He was waving us on from the top of the fence.

People filed in behind us, blocking off the last cop, chanting and howling, pushing us forward while the cop got farther and farther away, tangled up in the mob.

Rahmer climbed down, we went through the fence, made our way into the crowd on the street. Moving through the mob, Rahmer started touching people, grabbing their hands and shaking them, squeezing the tops of their arms, patting their shoulders, like we were all in on something together.

Me, I just kept moving, weaving through the crowd, thinking how much easier it all would've been if no one had ever gotten their hands on each other—or if Ortiz had known his birth mother, or if I were taller, or if fall wasn't coming, and then the summer again . . .

I could hear the blasts getting louder behind me, and the drums kicking in harder—the big-bang grand finale, but I didn't need to turn around to see it, I knew what it looked like. It was just another version of the old thing, the noise, the circles of fire, one stretching out in another.

When Ortiz died, I'd begged Livia to come back. When the second twin died, I'd begged her harder. When Rahmer and Cali dropped me off home, I called her again, I told her, "Don't come back—there's nothing we can do for each other."

"Sweetie, no."

"We're just the same thing over and over again."

"Listen to me, Leon, listen to me."

"We can't talk our way through it."

"Listen to me," she said, "listen—you need me. You said so. You said you'd make it right."

"But you hate me, Livia."

"Oh, sweetie—no. I still love you. Despite what you did to me."

Her voice was dead, flat, but I wasn't scared of her.

"I love you too. I didn't do anything."

"I almost killed myself for you."

"No you didn't, not for me."

"There are worse things I could have done to you than just break up with you."

"I know."

"You were supposed to be my slave."

"I know. It was the wrong move."

"When it comes to men," she said, "there are dogs and there is dogshit. Guess which one you are."

"Good."

"Listen," she said, "listen," but I was hanging up.

I went around the apartment taking the appliances out of the towels I'd wrapped them in, plugged them all into their sockets, sat on the floor and listened—they were humming back to life.

When the dark went cool blue I was still there, I heard garbage trucks down in the street, taking things away, leaf blowers scattering cut grass into the gutters, and any second there'd be another black spot, another cat, some dark flurry jumping at me out of nowhere. There was no ducking them.

They came from that place Dara was always watching with her magic eye, that place where she found the Lord, where Livia found her asteroid, that place that had Ortiz—and me too, soon enough.

I was waiting my turn through the emptiness, the slash in the color of the world.

IAN SPIEGELMAN was born in Brooklyn in 1974 and raised in Bayside, Queens. A graduate of Queens College and a former staff writer for *New York,* he is currently a reporter for the *New York Post*'s Page Six and a contributing editor at *Details.* He lives in Forest Hills, Queens. For more information, visit www.everyonesburning.com